WOLF BLOOD

Wild City

SHARON GOSLING

Piccadilly
PRESS

For Isla and Emily

First published in Great Britain in 2016 by
PICCADILLY PRESS
80–81 Wimpole St, London W1G 9RE
www.piccadillypress.co.uk

Text copyright © Piccadilly Press, 2016

Wolfblood copyright © BBC 2012 and ZDFE 2012

Based on the series created by Debbie Moon

A CIP catalogue record for this book is available from the British Library.

ISBN: 978-1-84812-547-6
also available as an ebook

1

Typeset by Palimpsest Book Production Ltd, Falkirk, Stirlingshire

Printed and bound by Clays Ltd, St Ives Plc

Piccadilly Press is an imprint of Bonnier Publishing Fiction,
a Bonnier Publishing company
www.bonnierpublishingfiction.co.uk
www.bonnierpublishing.co.uk

One

The city of Newcastle glinted in the night, light rioting with noise and colour on every street and along every bustling path. The place was as alive as she was, Jana thought, a strange creature in and of itself, people and cars moving along its streets like blood cells rushing and bumping through the veins of a body. The young Wolfblood slipped into an alley and stood still in the shadows. She sniffed, listening carefully. There was a game on at St James's Park; she could hear the roar of the crowd in the stands and the thump of the ball as it smashed against a goal post. A breeze was rippling the nearby waters of the Tyne, the brackish salt tang of the estuary washing to her through the noisy dark.

The scent that she had been following had been swallowed by a million other smells. Jana tried to filter out everything except a single body amid all this human chaos: the one person for whom she was searching . . .

She blinked, thwarted and frustrated. Even in this relatively quiet alley the clamour was too much. She couldn't find her quarry. Jana touched the earpiece that connected her to Segolia headquarters and then spoke to the woman she knew was waiting on the other end of the line.

'Imara, I think I've lost him,' Jana said, loud enough for her earpiece to pick up the words. 'He's gone. He's *good*.'

'He is,' agreed the voice of Imara Cipriani. 'But you're better.'

Jana smiled. That was high praise indeed from Segolia's alpha. Jana centred herself and concentrated.

Another minute and there it was – a scent now so familiar that she knew it at once. 'Got him!'

'And that,' Imara's voice said into her ear, 'is why you're our best agent.'

Jana smiled to herself and headed out of the dark alley, stepping from the relative calm into the full flow of a city street. She hesitated, taking a deep breath as Newcastle's bustle buffeted her. So many humans all crushed together, so much noise – it was still new to her, this kind of life, this kind of place. It was overwhelming, sometimes.

'Jana?' Imara asked, alert to her hesitation. 'What's going on?'

'I'm here,' Jana said, shaking herself. 'I know where he's going. Wolfbloods always head for familiar territory . . .'

She raced through the crowds, heading for the Kafe. Jana wasn't the only Bradlington High student who had found their way to the big city. Katrina's dad had found her the perfect city site down by the river – and that's

2

exactly where Jana was headed. Because that's where TJ would be. TJ, the wayward Wolfblood who should have been home at six p.m. sharp.

Imara's son.

Jana walked through the door of the Kafe just in time to catch a flying cup before it smashed into the window beside her. She looked across the room to see a tall, athletic boy of about sixteen standing on a table. One of the Kafe's chairs was on its back at his feet, evidently because he had tried – and failed – to perform some kind of daring balancing act on it. The fallen chair had crashed on to a tray that had once held the cup that had been catapulted into Jana's hand.

TJ Cipriani looked distinctly sheepish, probably because on its trip across the room, the cup had emptied its contents all over the pretty girl he'd no doubt been trying to impress. Jana shook her head. *TJ*. Always looking for the joke. It was annoying that she never managed to stay mad at him for long. No one did, not even Imara, for all her hard-as-nails Segolia executive exterior. He was just . . . TJ.

'Nice catch, Jana,' called Katrina, from behind the counter. 'The usual?'

'Thanks, but I've got to get *Terence* home.' She raised her eyebrows at the Wolfblood across the room.

TJ sighed and followed her out of the door, hauling his backpack over his shoulder. His skateboard was strapped to it, just as it always was. Sometimes Jana thought TJ's board was as much a part of him as were his arms and his legs.

'It's *TJ*,' he insisted, as they made their way along the river, 'and you're supposed to be on my side.'

'I am!'

'Then why are you playing fetch for my mum? Just because you work for her –'

'With her,' Jana corrected him quickly.

'– doesn't mean you have to be her lapdog at home, too.'

'Lapdog?' Jana snarled, eyes yellowing as she turned on him. He was head and shoulders taller than she was but since when had that made a difference to an angry Wolfblood?

TJ gave a cheeky grin, his hazel eyes sparkling. 'Now that's the wild I'm looking for!'

Jana sighed, letting her wolf fade again. She'd only been in Newcastle for a few months, and the move from Stoneybridge hadn't been easy. Out of everyone she had known at school, only the Three Ks – Katrina, Kay and Kara – were also in the city. Rhydian was deep in the wilds of Canada with Maddy, Shannon was immersed in her Segolia-funded university course down south, and Tom was at college, putting his love of football to use as he trained to be a coach. Jana had promised Segolia she'd work with the company's Wolfblood employees to

4

pass on some of her wild Wolfblood knowledge to the city pack. Imara had convinced her that Segolia needed Jana's insight and skills – that the city and wild packs should be more connected. They were all Wolfbloods, after all. Jana had felt that she at least needed to try. She'd seen for herself that Wolfbloods and humans could live together as friends. Surely all Wolfbloods should be able to do the same?

Imara and TJ had done their best to help her fit in. Imara had even given Jana a place to live – a room in her comfortable home, which was where she and TJ were headed right now.

'It's not easy for me, TJ,' she told him. 'Fitting into all this.'

'That's why you should be on my side!' said TJ, throwing up his hands. 'You and me, we're beasts of the night, running free! At least I'm living by my own rules.'

'No one really lives by their own rules,' Jana pointed out. 'Not even in the wild. The pack, your family, Segolia – there's always someone –' She stopped, sniffing the air as a scent distracted her. 'Wolfbloods!'

A moment later, two wolves appeared, racing down the street in full view of every human around. Cars screeched to a halt, but the creatures just kept going.

'That's what I'm talking about!' yelled TJ. 'Running wild, Wolfblood-style!'

Jana watched as a sinister-looking black van raced

after the fleeing Wolfbloods. She took off after them, TJ close on her heels.

'Oh no,' Jana muttered. 'Call your mum,' she shouted to TJ, as she started to run, 'tell her what's happening!'

Jana chased after the van at Wolfblood speed. She dodged through streets, realising that they were heading for a quiet, industrial part of the river. The smell of salt was strong in the air, metal mixed with oil, too. The van pulled in through the gates of a dark, silent boatyard and Jana skidded to a halt outside, hanging back so she wouldn't be seen. She heard the van pull to a stop inside, hidden from view by the large, silent ranks of boats berthed close together in dry dock.

'Did you call her?' Jana asked TJ, as he caught up.

'She says to stay put,' he whispered.

Jana had no intention of doing that. She ducked in through the gates.

TJ threw up his hands in frustration. 'And I thought *I* was the one who couldn't take orders!'

Jana dodged the puddles that had collected on the rough ground inside the yard, keeping to the shadows. Boats of all sizes rested on trailers large and small, casting strangely shaped shadows along the narrow avenues that cut between them. Jana sniffed, trying to locate the Wolfbloods. Shouts echoed in the distance but she still couldn't see either of them – or whoever had been driving the van.

TJ caught up with her and Jana shushed him before he

6

could speak, pushing him deeper into the shadows. Ahead, a flashlight sliced through the darkness, obviously searching for the Wolfbloods. She waited until it moved on and then slipped out of her hiding place. TJ went to go with her, but she pushed him back again, trying to force him to stay put. She didn't want anything to happen to him, not when Imara was on her way. Jana could handle this herself.

'Wait!' TJ called after her, in a loud but nervous whisper. 'We can't split up! It's always the cool black kid that gets grabbed first!'

Jana didn't stop. She slipped from shadow to shadow, silent and quick. Then she turned a corner and came face to face with one of the Wolfbloods. He was a boy of about her age, with an untidy mop of thick dark hair and anxious eyes. They yellowed as he saw Jana, his veins running black as he snarled.

Jana's first instinct was to snarl back, but she raised her hands instead, trying to placate him. 'Easy,' she said. 'I'm here to help . . .'

There came a sound, very close – the terrified yelp of an animal in fear.

'Emilia!' the boy shouted, barging past Jana and slipping into the darkness.

Jana ran after him, sliding to a stop as she found herself in an open space formed by a gap in the cars, far better lit and with fewer places to hide. In the centre of the space lay a female wolf. A figure holding a rifle stood opposite, and before Jana could react, the Wolfblood boy leapt at him, snarling.

'No!' Jana shouted, as the sound of a shot echoed sharply out of the dark.

TJ appeared at her side, staring in horror at the two downed wolves as the person with the gun calmly stepped forward.

'Stand back,' said the man. 'Wolves are dangerous.'

It was then that Jana saw the cages that were standing in the back of the open van. The two Wolflbloods were tranquillised, then – not dead. At least that was something.

'Who are you?' she snapped. 'The police?'

The man shook his head. 'I'm a vet from Northumbria Animal Park,' he said. 'This is for their own good. Wild animals don't belong in the city.'

Jana made an angry growling sound. 'They don't belong behind bars, either!'

The man frowned. 'Should you be in here?'

'We – er . . . we're big animal lovers,' TJ told him, tugging at her sleeve. 'And we're just leaving. Yeah? Come on, Jana . . .'

TJ dragged her away towards the gate before she could wolf out completely. They'd just made it out of the boatyard when the van drove past. Jana watched it go, fury sparking the wolf in her veins.

'We're letting my mum handle this now, right?' TJ said hopefully.

Jana shook her head. 'They can't wait that long. I know what it's like to be locked in a cage.'

TJ grabbed her arm, trying to hold her back. 'Look, Jana. This isn't Kincaid –'

She turned on him with a snarl, angry that he'd even utter that name. How could TJ possibly know anything about what she'd seen Alexander Kincaid try to do? He'd developed a serum that would strip Wolfbloods of their nature and turn them entirely human. Not only that, the first pack he'd targeted had been Jana's. How could TJ ever understand what it was like to know that your entire pack was in danger? These two young Wolfbloods – whoever they were – needed just as much help as her father or Aran and Meinir had. She'd felt helpless then, unable to do anything. Jana had vowed she'd never feel that way ever again. She wasn't helpless. She was a Wolfblood, an *alpha*, and she'd help other Wolfbloods in any way she could.

Jana shook TJ off, wrenching her arm away. Then she ran after the van.

Two

Jana knew exactly where the animal park was. She'd been appalled to find out that there was a zoo right inside the city, hemmed in by concrete buildings and busy streets. She avoided even walking past it, hating to hear the echoing calls of the creatures trapped within. Now, though, she made straight for the entrance: double gates edged by towering brick walls that had been painted a stark, slick white. The gates were shut and locked, the whole place in darkness. Jana stalked to the wall and looked up. There was a CCTV camera perched on top of it, far above her head. She watched as every few minutes the device scanned left and right, surveying the street outside. Jana made sure she stood just outside the scope of its vision as the sound of running footsteps echoed behind her.

'Stay here,' she said, as TJ appeared. 'Wait for your mum.'

'You're not going in there alone,' he declared. 'You need my street smarts and mad skillz!'

Jana grabbed TJ's arm as he made for the wall, pulling him back. 'Let's keep the "mad skillz" off-camera, OK?'

TJ looked up at the wall and made a face. He hadn't

even seen the camera. Jana moved away, searching for somewhere safer to climb. In just a few minutes, they were both inside.

Park is the wrong name for this place, Jana thought. *Hell would be a better description . . .* Rows of large cages had been set along narrow pathways for human visitors to walk along. Animal smells bombarded her from every angle, and everywhere she looked there were bars. She was surrounded. It almost felt as if she were inside a cage herself.

'Cages,' she whispered, panic rising in her gut. 'C-c-c-cages . . .'

TJ put his hand on her arm, bringing her back to her senses. 'You're all right,' he said. 'Stay with me, OK? Come on.'

They moved through the zoo, avoiding the CCTV cameras. Ahead of them, a row of low, flat-roofed buildings loomed out of the darkness, all painted the same clinical white.

Jana glanced at TJ, then cocked her head at a door in front of them. On it were the words 'Security Control Room'. They headed for a window and peered inside. Row upon row of monitors stood in front of a control desk, displaying CCTV from every area of the park. There was a woman inside, wearing the outfit of a security guard. She was simpering at a man that they both recognised as the vet who had captured the Wolfbloods. The security guard got up to make tea as the vet looked at a screen. On it were the images of two sleeping wolves. They lay in separate cages set side by side.

'These two have been wild in the city for weeks,' came his muffled voice. 'Anything could have happened to them. They'll be safe here.'

Jana pulled TJ away from the window.

'But where are their cages?' TJ whispered, sniffing. 'There are too many other scents – I can't tell . . .'

Jana didn't answer. She led TJ to one of the trees planted in the square. Crouching at its base, she pressed one hand against the ground. She slipped into Eolas, the wild Wolfblood state that connected her to all of nature. Its golden edges sparked, awareness rippling through her as her heightened senses let Jana see the park from all angles. She found the two Wolfbloods, sleeping peacefully in their enclosures. She stepped out of Eolas again, now sure of exactly where they were.

'This way,' she said quietly.

'How come you get spidey-sense and I don't?' TJ asked.

Jana raised one eyebrow. 'Well, if you'd paid more attention to my lessons . . .'

TJ looked as if he was about to argue, and then shrugged. 'Fair point.'

Jana watched the panning cameras, waiting for a clear moment. When the nearest one swung away, she started running. 'Come on!'

One of the Wolfbloods was still out for the count when they found them, but the other was beginning to stir. Jana went for one of the doors, but TJ held her back, nodding at yet another camera that was pointed at the cages. He counted as it swung back again.

'They're out of sight for twenty seconds,' he whispered.

They waited until the camera moved again, then dashed to the bars. In the time it had taken for them to get there, one of the Wolfbloods – the boy that had confronted Jana – had transformed back into a human. He was stirring, but not fully awake.

'Wake up!' Jana hissed through the bars. 'Time to go!'

'What?' muttered the boy and then, as his dark eyes slowly focused, he muttered, 'TJ?'

'I thought it was you!' said TJ. 'Jana, meet Matei Covaci. We go to the same school. He's Year Eleven's Mister Popular. *Not.*' TJ nodded at the still-sleeping wolf. 'This furball is your little sis, right?'

Matei turned to look at the wolf in the cage beside him. 'Emilia! Emilia, wake up!' He rattled at the bars that separated him from his sister. 'Get her out, now!'

'We're going to get you both out,' Jana told him.

'Five seconds!' TJ warned her.

'Wolf form – now!' Jana ordered Matei. She and TJ dashed out of view as the camera panned back around. Matei only just managed to transform in time.

'Wait here,' Jana whispered to TJ. Before he had time

to argue, she slipped back to the buildings where the vet was monitoring the wolves. They had passed another door, one that said 'Maintenance'. Breaking in as quickly and quietly as she could, Jana grabbed a toolbox from one of the workbenches and slipped back to where TJ waited, just in time for the camera to move away again.

A split-second later they were both back at the bars of Matei's cage.

'Hurry up and get my sister out,' he hissed.

Jana ignored him, focusing instead on using a screwdriver. She couldn't pick the lock, but she could remove it completely . . .

'Wild Wolfblood,' TJ grinned. 'Big on the ingenuity.'

Matei wasn't impressed. 'Well, tell your wild girlfriend to get Emilia out first.'

Jana looked at TJ. 'Your *what*?'

TJ looked horrified. 'I never said girlfriend. I never said that!' he glanced up. 'Camera!'

It was only when Jana had reached cover that she realised she'd left the toolbox behind. The camera passed over it and she was sure the vet and the security guard would come running.

But they didn't.

Another few seconds and they were back at the cage.

'What were you doing wolfing out in the city anyway?' Jana asked Matei.

'None of your business,' the boy said sulkily.

TJ made a sound in his throat. 'Says the boy we're saving from a locked cage . . .'

The last screw came away. A second later Matei was out and Jana got to work on Emilia's cage. The girl was starting to come round, and as the tranquilliser wore off she became her human form. She was small with long blonde hair – and had terrible burn scars all over her face.

'Matei?' Emilia said, scared.

Her brother moved to stand beside Jana. 'I'm right here.'

'I'll have you out in a minute,' Jana said, to the terrified girl. To Matei she said, 'Stay in the cage. For the camera.'

'I'm staying with my sister. TJ can play wolf.'

'Do you want the guys with guns here?' Jana barked. 'Get in the cage!'

Matei did as he was told. The camera began to move back again. Jana and TJ rushed out of the way, but Emilia didn't wolf out.

'Transform!' Jana told her, from the shadows. 'Quickly!'

The camera panned over her, still human, and Jana's heart banged in her chest. She looked towards the security control centre.

'Emilia – you have to transform!'

The girl did, just in time for the camera to pass over her again as it moved back. There was no movement from the security office. Jana breathed a sigh of relief. She got the cage door open, but Emilia was too scared to leave.

15

'Emilia,' Matei coaxed, getting into the cage with her, 'it's all right . . .'

'Camera!' said TJ.

It was too late. Jana and TJ managed to get out of sight, but there was no chance that the two people in the control room wouldn't notice that the captive wolves had been replaced by two kids!

'Run!' Jana yelled. 'Everyone just run!'

TJ wasn't fast enough. He turned as he heard the camera swing around again, catching his face full in its sights. He caught up with Jana as the four of them ran for the perimeter. 'They got me. I'm on camera. I've got to find that footage and wipe it.'

'Segolia will sort it out.'

'Yeah, and then Mum will sort *me* out!' He ran back.

'What is he doing?' Matei exclaimed as TJ disappeared into the darkness.

'Get your sister out of here,' Jana told him.

'But –'

'Go!' Jana shouted over her shoulder, already running after TJ.

She doubled back through the park, catching up with TJ just as the vet left the control room with the tranquilliser gun. That just left the guard inside. They could hear her trying to direct the vet from the CCTV screens.

'I'll deal with her.' Jana transformed and headed for the door, slipping inside.

16

'H-hello?' the guard turned and Wolf-Jana moved towards her, snarling. The woman was brave enough to stand her ground for about five seconds before fleeing for the door.

TJ appeared a moment later, a grin plastered on his face. 'Job done!'

'Not yet,' Jana told him, pointing at the control desk. 'Any idea how any of this works?'

'Leave it to the expert,' TJ said confidently. He sat down and hit a button, which turned all the lights in the park on in one go in a blinding glare of light. He hurriedly hit the button again, turning them off. 'Oops. This one . . .' He tried another, and ridiculous jolly music began to blare out from loudspeakers.

'TJ!'

'Got it!' TJ said, punching another button and pointing to the screen in front of him.

DELETE ALL CCTV RECORDINGS? YES/NO

TJ hit 'YES' and a progress bar popped up.

50% DELETED . . . 70% DELETED . . . 90% DELETED . . .

'Go!' he yelled, scooting out of the chair so fast he left the wheels spinning as they bolted for the door.

They'd made it out of the control room when the vet reappeared, still holding the tranquilliser gun. Jana looked at TJ. This time they really were caught.

Then sounds echoed out of the darkness close by –

howling, keening. Wolves! The vet spun around, trying to see them, but they were just fluid shapes in the shadows.

TJ and Jana made a run for it, heading for the perimeter as fast as they could. Matei and Emilia joined them, back in human form, and together the four Wolfbloods climbed the wall.

Jana thought they'd made it, but as they dropped to the ground, the harsh lights of a big car flared into life. The four Wolfbloods stood, rooted to the ground as a figure stepped out.

There was a moment of silence.

'Hi, Mum,' said TJ.

Imara just crossed her arms and stared at them all, a look of utter disappointment on her face.

The next day the four Wolfbloods met up at the Kafe. Katrina wasn't in the best of moods. Kay was supposed to be living with her in the flat upstairs, but she'd found another room closer to college. Jana could tell Katrina was upset. Jana understood – she missed her friends, too. Tom and Shannon were so busy that she hadn't seen them for ages and who knew when she'd see Rhydian again . . . if she ever did.

'It's OK,' she said to Katrina, trying to cheer her up. 'Friends are forever, however far away they might be.'

'Yeah,' Katrina agreed. 'Ooh, new customers,' she added, as the door opened and Matei and Emilia walked in. They were closely followed by TJ. Katrina's face turned into a scowl. 'Stay away from my furniture, TJ!'

'This welcoming lady is Katrina,' TJ told Matei and Emilia. 'She owns the Kafe.'

'It's nice,' Emilia said, looking around. 'Colourful.'

Katrina grinned. 'A young lady with taste! We're going to be friends, I can tell. Welcome to the Kafe.'

TJ ordered drinks while the other three went to sit down. At school, Matei had asked TJ to get a message to Jana, saying that he and Emilia urgently needed help. Now he pushed a gold ring across the table, his dark eyes serious.

'It was our mother's. It was found after the fire. It started in Dad's study,' Matei explained. 'The whole house was alight in minutes, there just wasn't time . . .'

Jana glanced at Emilia's scarred face, suddenly realising what must have happened to put the scars there. She swallowed. Fire – every Wolfblood's worst nightmare. 'You were trapped inside?'

'I got Emilia out through a window,' Matei went on. 'Just. She still wakes up in the night yelling. And the way people stare at her . . .'

'Your parents?' Jana asked softly. Matei didn't say anything, just shook his head. Jana's heart clenched and she reached out, taking his hand. He squeezed back, gently, as if grateful for the support.

'We don't have any other family,' Matei went on, his

voice quiet. 'Only an aunt and uncle who we've never met – they live in Romania. So we're with a foster family now. And . . . and we want to know,' he said, his voice threatening to break. 'We want to know what really happened. Segolia looked into it. The police, too. They say it was an accident.'

'Matei, I trust Segolia,' Jana said. 'I wouldn't work for them if I didn't.'

'They could have missed something,' Emilia pointed out. 'With your wild Wolfblood abilities, you can find things they didn't.'

TJ arrived with their drinks as Jana thought about it. 'I'll talk to Imara,' she said.

Emilia shook her head. 'No. You have to do it alone.'

'We trust you,' Matei told her, fixing her with a serious look. 'Just you.'

'That's my mum you're talking about!' TJ said indignantly. 'She's spent her whole life helping Wolfbloods. Jana, tell them!'

'Jana,' Emilia begged. 'Please.'

Jana bit her lip. How could she refuse such a request? She knew what it was like to need answers. Eventually she nodded slowly and picked up the ring, feeling its weight in her hand. 'We need to go somewhere quiet,' she said. 'And as wild as we can find, in the city.'

'The wilderness park,' Matei suggested. 'It's not far.'

*　　*　　*

20

It was awful. Even worse than she'd imagined. The fear, the heat . . . The fire flickered around her, shadows burning, smoke choking . . . Jana writhed in Ansion, the Wolfblood sense that allowed her to connect to the past. She could hear Emilia crying out for her parents as if Jana were standing right there herself, stuck in that house with them as the fire raged all around . . .

'Jana,' came TJ's voice, from very far away. 'That's enough. Stop!'

She hunched away from him, clutching the ring, forcing herself to keep going. The memories licked at her as surely as the flames. Jana fought her way through them, gasping for air . . . She looked for a way out. There was a window, and beyond it . . . Was that . . . ?

'Jana!' TJ yelled, grabbing her arm. 'Come back!'

She gasped, flung out of Ansion, out of the past and back into the present. Crouching, hunched beside the crumbling ruins of a stone folly that stood over the city, Jana looked up at Matei and Emilia.

'What did you see?' Emilia asked.

'A face,' she managed. 'At the window. Outside, looking in. A boy.'

'A Wolfblood?' Matei asked.

Jana shook her head. 'No.'

'A human!' Matei exclaimed. 'Did he start the fire?'

TJ helped Jana to her feet. 'I don't know, Matei,' she said. 'I just know he was there.'

'So we find him,' said Emilia.

'Jana,' TJ begged. 'You should take this to Segolia. Tell my mum.'

'No,' said Matei firmly. 'You'll help us, won't you, Jana? To find out the truth?'

Jana looked at them all. 'Do I have any choice?' she asked.

Three

Although she'd told Matei and Emilia that she wouldn't go to Segolia about what she'd seen, Jana knew that she had to at least use the corporation's resources. Since starting to work with Segolia, Jana had realised just how big the company was, not to mention what advanced technology they had. She had her own security access to most of their computer systems. So, early the next morning, sitting in the kitchen in Imara's spotless home, Jana accessed the Segolia archive. Her aim: to find some information about what had happened to Matei and Emilia's parents.

She'd been reading for a while when she caught a scent behind her.

'Don't even think about it,' she said, aloud, to the hopeless individual attempting to sneak up on her.

TJ appeared at her side with a long-suffering sigh. 'I can never get one over on you.'

'Maybe you should sneak up on me when I'm not hiding something?' she suggested, tilting the laptop away as he tried to see the screen.

TJ huffed. 'Nice to be trusted. Why don't you just ask my mum about the Covacis?'

'I did,' Jana admitted, feeling slightly guilty that she'd done exactly what she'd promised she wouldn't to Matei and Emilia. Not that it had got her anywhere: Imara had shrugged off her questions. 'She said digging around in the past "would unsettle" Matei and Emilia.'

'She's not wrong,' TJ muttered, and then shrugged at the disapproving look Jana gave him. 'They're not exactly the poster kids for stability, are they?'

'Or maybe there's something Imara doesn't want me to know?'

'Yeah,' TJ scoffed, 'like the UFO she has parked in the garage and Big Foot stashed in the shed . . .'

Jana turned the laptop around so he could see the screen and opened a file.

'I found this at the end of the report on the fire.'

TJ frowned as he read off the screen. '"Action taken: Protocol Five." Sounds cool. What is it?'

'I don't know,' Jana told him. 'I've searched for it repeatedly, but I keep getting an "Access Denied" symbol.'

'I thought you had access to all areas?'

'So did I. So why is she hiding things from me?'

TJ didn't have an answer for that. Jana started to make breakfast.

'Are you going to ask my mum?' TJ asked. 'I thought the point of Segolia was that you're all on the same side. Wolfbloods Assemble.'

Jana flipped a piece of bacon. 'I'll ask her when –'

'Ask me what?' Imara asked, appearing behind them, dressed as always in a perfectly tailored outfit, her glossy dark hair as immaculate as her subtle, businesslike make-up. Jana had no idea how Imara managed it. She was the kind of woman who would never have a single hair out of place, even if she found herself standing in the path of a tornado. An aura of cold efficiency emanated from her every pore. 'By the way, Norway's off.'

'What?' TJ burst out. He'd been looking forward to their full moon trip all month. 'Why?'

'Hmm, let me think,' said his mother. 'Wolves on the streets, breaking into the animal park –'

'We saved the day, and we get punished?' TJ said, outraged.

'I told you to wait,' Imara replied. 'You're both lucky you're spending the night in the cellar, and not being shipped off to Siberia!'

'But what if this is it?' TJ asked. 'You promised my first time would be in the mountains!'

His mum looked him up and down. 'You look flushed. Could be a fever?'

TJ frowned. 'I'm fine.'

'Any dizziness?'

'No! Honest, Mum, nothing.'

Jana suppressed a smile. She knew exactly what Imara was doing. TJ's mum smiled at her cub sweetly.

'Well, then you won't be transforming tonight, will you?'

TJ was not happy. 'Fine! I'm off to school!'

'Er – breakfast?' Jana reminded him as he flounced away.

'Give it to Big Foot!'

Imara sighed as TJ left. 'There's something seriously wrong with that boy. So, what did you want to ask me?'

Jana forced a smile. 'Nothing,' she said.

A big part of Jana's job at Segolia was trying to teach the city Wolfbloods the skills they had forgotten. The company had provided a dedicated space in which she could give lessons in skills that were part of their natural birthright. The room was an oasis inside Segolia's efficient office block, full of plants and even carpeted with lush grass so that the city Wolfbloods could escape from the concrete jungle outside and immerse themselves in nature. Here, Jana did her best to teach them about Eolas – it was a sense that came naturally to wild Wolfbloods, but had been almost completely lost by the city-borns. Showing them how to access that part of themselves wasn't easy.

Jana, disappointed after another fruitless session, dismissed her latest class.

'It's full moon tonight,' she said to Imara, who hadn't fared any better than her employees. 'If they can't access Eolas today . . . I promised Victoria we'd have mastered Eolas by now –'

Imara scowled at the mention of Segolia's security chief.

Jana wasn't surprised that the two women weren't the best of friends. Victoria Sweeney wasn't the easiest person to know. She took her duties involving keeping Wolfbloods secret from the rest of the world incredibly seriously. Coupled with a personality that seemed to be naturally abrasive and suspicious, Sweeney didn't have many close friends. But she had helped the wild Wolfbloods when they had needed her. Jana couldn't forget that.

'Victoria isn't the alpha here any more,' Imara reminded her. 'And I say you're doing fine. I trust you.'

Jana looked at her. 'Do you?'

'Yes.'

'Then what's Protocol Five?' At Imara's surprised look, Jana rushed on. 'I did Ansion for Matei and Emilia. I saw the fire that killed their parents. And someone else was there, looking in the window. A boy our age, a human. I checked the file, but there was nothing about any boy. Just "Action taken: Protocol Five".'

Imara sighed. 'It's an instruction to get rid of evidence. Anything left in the wreckage that might have exposed the Covacis as Wolfbloods.'

'Why don't I have clearance?' Jana asked.

'What Segolia does to protect the secret isn't always legal,' Imara explained. 'We were trying to protect you.'

'What if the fire wasn't an accident?' Jana asked. 'What if this boy started it?'

Imara shook her head. 'We investigated thoroughly.'

'But you never knew he was there,' Jana pointed out. 'What was he doing looking in the window? What did he see? If they wolfed out during the fire and he saw, then I'd say we've got a serious problem. Wouldn't you?'

Imara paused for a minute, thinking. 'OK,' she said. 'Do you think you saw enough of his face for me to develop a photofit?'

Jana nodded. 'I think so.'

'Come to my office, then. We'll work on it now.'

Jana followed Imara to the large, comfortable office where Segolia's alpha spent a lot of her time. They sat side by side on the black leather sofa as Imara opened Segolia's image-building programme. They began to piece together a picture of the face that Jana had seen at the window.

'His nose was narrower,' Jana said a few minutes later, frowning at the picture of the thin white face that they had generated. 'Eyebrows a bit heavier . . . Yeah. That's him, more or less. He could be a neighbour, someone Matei and Emilia might recognise.'

'All right,' nodded Imara, sending the image to Jana's own iPad via Bluetooth. 'Report back to me as soon as you've spoken to them. And keep them in line – I don't want a repeat of the other night, especially on a full moon.'

Jana went straight to Hawthorn Secondary School, the large city comprehensive TJ, Matei and Emilia all attended. She sat on the low wall outside the entrance, waiting for them as they came out of lessons at the end of the day.

'You told Segolia?' Matei asked immediately, a look of wary accusation in his eyes.

'I told TJ's mum,' Jana corrected him. 'We can trust her. Here's the boy I saw.' She held up the iPad.

'That looks like Darren,' TJ said, as they all gathered around. 'That boy who was expelled?'

'Yeah,' agreed Matei. 'I recognise him.'

'Expelled for what?' Jana asked. 'When?'

'He came into school at two a.m.,' TJ elaborated. 'He tagged all over the place.'

'Three weeks after the fire,' Matei added.

'Where does he live?' Jana asked.

TJ shook his head. 'I don't know. But I know someone who does.'

He led them to the school gym, where a girl in a colourful hijab was using a punchbag to go through an impressive series of kickboxing moves. Powerful and graceful, Jana could tell immediately that the girl was a Wolfblood.

'That's Selina Khan,' TJ said quietly. 'Let me talk to her. I've known her for years. She's the lone wolf type.' He moved forward as the others hung back.

'Hey, Selina,' TJ tried. 'How's it going?'

The girl glanced at him, not even out of breath. 'What do you want, TJ?'

'Remember Darren? He bullied you last year.'

'*Tried* to bully me,' she corrected.

'Didn't your parents march you round to his place to apologise?'

Selina frowned. 'Why do you want to know?'

'We need his address.'

She stared at the pen and paper he was holding out, and shrugged. 'If it'll get rid of you, sure. Unless,' Selina added, grinning as she wrote down the details and handed it back, 'you want to spar?'

TJ backed away, quickly. He was no match for Selina in full flow. He knew it and so did she. Selina smiled to herself and went back to her training.

'OK,' said Jana. 'I'll go round, check it's the boy I saw.'

'Not without us,' Matei told her, grabbing the address from TJ.

'You're joking,' said TJ. 'It's full moon!'

'This is about our parents,' Emilia pointed out. 'He might have started the fire!'

'We just want to see him for ourselves,' added Matei.

Jana sighed. 'TJ, you go home and tell Imara –'

TJ cut her off. 'Not gonna happen, wild girl. We stick together, right?'

Jana looked at him. 'You just don't want to be the one who tells your mum, do you?'

He shrugged. 'Do you blame me?'

Jana shook her head. 'Fine. But we do it my way.'

Four

It was easy enough to find the street and then the home in question, one of a modest line of detached red-brick houses built in blocks of two with a small, neatly kept garden in the front and a narrow path leading around the side. Jana made Matei and Emilia wait at the road-side as she and TJ knocked on the door. A figure came down the hallway towards them, distorted by the stained-glass panel. As soon as it opened and she saw the pale, narrow face of the thin boy in front of them Jana knew it matched both her photofit picture and the memory of him in her head.

'Yeah?' said Darren, standing in the open doorway.

'It's him,' Jana said to TJ.

She'd said it quietly, but Emilia still heard. The girl had been coiled as tightly as a spring since they had decided to come here, and at Jana's words, she launched herself down the path towards the house with an angry, snarling yell.

'Emilia!' Matei shouted, running after her as she pushed between Jana and TJ and shoved Darren back into the house, her fingers clawing at his throat.

'What did you do?' Emilia shouted, as Darren tried to get away. 'What did you *do*?'

Jana grabbed her, dragging Emilia back from the winded boy before he could see how yellow her eyes had turned.

'She's off her head!' Darren hissed. 'Get out! I haven't done *nothin*'!'

'So why were you outside our house the night of the fire?' Matei asked, over the struggling Emilia's head. They were all crammed into the doorway, facing off against Darren.

An expression of panic passed over Darren's face, but before anyone could say anything else, a voice floated out to them from another room.

'Darren?'

Everyone froze.

'Go!' whispered Jana. 'All of you!' She pushed Matei and Emilia out of the door, pointing to the path beyond the garden. Matei pulled Emilia with him and TJ followed.

'What's going on?' called the voice, sounding worried.

Jana crossed her arms and raised an eyebrow at Darren. 'I can tell her about the fire, if you want?'

Darren glared at her, then raised his voice a little. 'Just someone from school, Mum.'

A small woman in a wheelchair appeared in the doorway. She looked up at Jana and they smiled at each other.

'Hi,' Jana said, as sweetly as she could. 'I'm Jana.'

The woman winked up at her son. Darren obviously

didn't get many visits from girls. 'Hello, Jana,' she said. 'I'm Tricia. You'll stay for tea?'

'I'd love to,' said Jana. She followed a reluctant Darren into the kitchen.

'I told him,' said Tricia, going to the table, 'don't get into trouble at school. Or you'll end up with no qualifications and no future, like his so-called friends. And then he does something stupid. For a dare!'

Jana sat down with her, looking around the kitchen as Darren made the tea. There was a stew bubbling on the stove and piles of carefully folded laundry on top of the washing machine. Everything was neat and tidy.

'Looks like he takes good care of you,' she said to Tricia.

Tricia nodded proudly. 'He's a good lad, really. I was in hospital that week. I tried to explain to the school how stressed he was but they expelled him. Anyway,' she said then, 'I'll leave you two to it . . .'

They watched her leave, and then Darren turned angrily to Jana. 'I had *nothin'* to do with that fire!'

'You were seen,' Jana told him.

'No, I wasn't. You're going to go. Or I'll call the police.'

'You really want the police here?'

'I've got nothing to hide,' Darren hissed. 'I feel terrible for them, a fire especially . . . But I wasn't there.'

Jana's heart ticked an extra beat. Had he known, then, that the people stuck inside were Wolfbloods? 'What d'you mean, "especially a fire"?'

He shrugged. 'Everyone's scared of fire.'

'Some more than others,' Jana pointed out. She watched him carefully. Her wolf senses told her he was really freaked out. There was definitely something he was hiding about that night.

Darren grabbed his phone. 'Nine . . . nine . . . nine . . .' he said deliberately, looking at her as he pressed the numbers, his thumb hovering over the 'call' button. '*Leave.*'

Jana gave up.

When she got outside, Jana sniffed and discovered that the others had slipped down the pathway that ran beside Darren and Tricia's house. Following, she found them all crouched against the brick wall, listening intently to what was going on inside. Jana concentrated on her wolf hearing, the sounds from within becoming amplified as she tuned into what her friends were listening to. Sound echoed to her as she heard Darren's voice. He was on the phone.

'Yeah, it's me,' he was saying. 'The kids I told you about, from the fire? They know I was there!'

There was a pause as the other person said something Jana couldn't quite catch, and then Darren's voice came again, 'All right. I'll see you there.' Then he hung up the phone and raised his voice. 'Mum? I'm going out!'

The four Wolfbloods crouched out of sight, watching as Darren left the house and headed down the street.

'He *was* there!' Matei hissed. 'We need to find out who he was talking to.'

'What if they're meeting after dark?' TJ pointed out. 'Clock's ticking, people! If we're still out when the moon rises . . .'

'I'm up for it if you are,' said Matei.

TJ made a face. 'Yeah – you're great at not getting caught . . .'

'Enough!' said Jana, exasperated at the bickering. 'If there's even a chance he knows the secret, we have to go after him. But we stay out of sight – and no matter what happens, we leave before moonrise.'

It was already heading towards evening by the time they had followed Darren to where he was meeting whoever had been on the other end of the line. He stopped on the footpath beneath the narrow railway bridge. The path crossed an area of scrubby wasteland. The four Wolfbloods had nowhere to hide, so they backed off and crouched next to the overgrown foliage further down the path, trusting the ever-lengthening shadows to keep them out of sight. Darren seemed nervous and miserable as he waited, checking both ways every few seconds to see if anyone was coming. TJ was nervous, too. Any minute now the moon would start to rise. If they were out in the open when that happened . . .

'Jana, c'mon,' he urged. 'Mum can sort this out Segolia-style tomorrow.'

But then two figures appeared, swaggering along the

path from the opposite direction. One was thin and weasely, wearing a hoodie. The other was bigger, with broad shoulders, wearing a baseball cap. They sauntered right up to where Darren stood.

'So what's all the panic, Darren?' asked the one in the cap. He stood with his beefy arms crossed as if he were spoiling for a fight.

'I told you,' Darren said, obviously nervous. 'Kids from school came to my house. This girl with them said I'd been seen. At the fire.'

The second boy loomed forward, right in Darren's face, threatening. 'And what did *you* say?'

'Nothing,' Darren told him. 'I swear.'

'If you said anything about us being there too . . .' the first boy warned.

Darren shook his head. 'I wouldn't do that. But if we went to the cops, said we were just hanging around –'

'No one is going to the cops!' barked the second boy, getting angry.

'Daz,' said his friend, soothingly. 'We didn't start that fire, and as long as you keep your mouth shut, the cops can't touch us for the other stuff, neither.'

The Wolfbloods looked at each other. If this wasn't about the fire, what *was* it about?

Something above them caught TJ's eye. He stared in horror at the full moon. It was rising, already right above them.

'Guys –' he began, but it was already too late.

Emilia was the first. She gasped, her body wracked with shaking. The girl looked down at her arms, seeing the veins blacken with Wolfblood. TJ gulped – they were out of time! But Darren and the two boys were showing no signs of leaving. If the Wolfbloods transformed here and now, they'd be seen for sure.

'TJ,' Jana managed, as her eyes yellowed, 'you'll have to do the talking!'

'Talking?' Matei asked, his veins bulging with Wolfbood as his eyes burned yellow. 'We're about to wolf out!'

Jana shook her head. 'TJ isn't.'

TJ flushed, embarrassed as Matei stared at him. He could see that Matei had realised what Jana meant. It wasn't that he'd been keeping the fact that he hadn't wolfed out yet a secret, exactly . . . he just didn't tend to tell people, that was all.

'Try not to screw this up!' Jana hissed at him, as her wolf-self consumed her.

The noise they were making had attracted the attention of Darren and the two thugs. They were taking out their phones and opening their torch apps, waving them around to see what was happening.

'What's that?' asked the one with the baseball cap. 'Who's there?'

TJ took a deep breath, and then, with his best swagger, walked out of the darkness, whistling as if he didn't have a care in the world.

37

'All right, lads?' he said. 'Fancy meeting you here.'

'That's TJ, from school,' said Darren. 'He's one of them.'

TJ grinned, terrified but doing his best to cover it. 'So which one of you three is going to tell me about the night of the fire?'

'Try talking to *this*,' said one of Darren's friends, raising his clenched fist.

'That doesn't even make sense,' TJ pointed out. 'I'm not the one doing the talking. Now if you'd said, "Try *listening* to this", at least that would have made sense. But you can't listen to a fist. I mean, what noise does a fist even make?'

'Let's find out,' snarled the other boy, as they both converged on TJ. Darren hung back, an anxious look on his face.

TJ stepped backwards, his heart beating fast. There was no way he'd come out on top if he had to fight these two on his own, wolf strength or no wolf strength. The boy with the baseball cap grinned, sensing an easy victory. He thumped a clenched fist into his opposite palm, ready for a fight.

Then a low, menacing growling sound filled the air. It stopped the two boys dead in their tracks.

A second later, the cocky looks on their faces were replaced by ones of total fear. The growling grew louder. Then out of the shadows slunk Jana, Matei and Emilia, all in wolf form. Their large, very sharp teeth were bared as they stalked into the meagre light, circling all three boys as if they were trapped sheep about to be ripped to pieces.

'Keep them dogs away from us!' One of them cringed, scared witless. 'It was Darren!'

'What was?' TJ demanded.

Darren kept his eyes on the wolves, shaking in his shoes. 'We robbed the house over the road,' he admitted. 'I saw the flames and went over to look. I heard howling – I – I thought there was a dog trapped inside. But I couldn't get in.' He looked at the other two, disgusted. 'They said we had to run. Then I heard the fire engine and I thought everything would be OK! I just wanted to save the dog . . .'

The wolves' growling lessened a little, but they continued to circle their quarry, giving them no chance to escape.

'Did you see how the fire started?' TJ asked.

Darren shook his head, still staring at the wolves, terrified.

'Anyone hanging around?'

'No! We didn't see nothin',' said Darren desperately. 'I couldn't get to them,' he added. 'I tried. I really tried . . .'

TJ blinked. Darren truly was upset, he realised. He wasn't a thug, like the other two. He'd just got in with the wrong crowd and didn't know how to deal with the guilt of it all.

'You two,' TJ said shortly to Darren's 'mates'. 'Go.'

They didn't need telling twice. The wolves parted just

a fraction and the two thugs scarpered through the gap, fleeing down the path and away into the darkness.

'And stay away from Darren!' TJ yelled after them.

'What did you say that for?' Darren asked, confused.

TJ shrugged. 'I've done you a favour. You should get some better friends. Now go home to your mum.'

Darren hesitated for a split-second. Then he ran, quickly vanishing into the gloom.

TJ looked at the Wolfbloods beside him, exasperated.

'Wolves on the streets *again*,' he said. 'My mum's gonna kill me . . .'

But before he'd even finished speaking, all three had taken off, out under the full moon, running as fast as they could.

'Hey!' he yelled. 'Wait for me!'

TJ found them the next morning, in the wilderness park. Emilia, Matei and Jana, back in human form, were sitting on a section of ruined wall with the city spread out below them. All three were munching happily on bacon sandwiches. TJ wished he'd been with them all night. They must have had a great time, whereas *he'd* had to go home and then sneak out again this morning while his mum was still in her basement den.

'At least you had a bed,' Matei pointed out, as TJ sat down between him and Emilia.

'Don't rub it in,' TJ complained.

Matei bumped his shoulder with a smile. 'Hey – maybe next month.'

TJ smiled back, glad of the encouragement. Matei was an all-right bloke, really, he decided.

'We should stay here forever,' Emilia sighed happily, looking around at the landscape that stretched wide and green in all directions. 'As wolves, living wild.'

TJ grinned and grabbed her sandwich. 'Well, if you're gonna be a *wild* wolf, you won't need this, will you?'

Emilia squealed and chased after him as he ran. They dodged in and out of the trees and bushes as Jana and Matei looked on. Jana smiled, but Matei seemed sad. He took out the chain he wore around his neck. On it was his mother's gold ring. He turned it in his fingers.

Jana reached out to touch it. 'Can I?' At his nod, she pressed it between her fingers, feeling Ansion rise up and wrap itself around her. Jana shut her eyes, letting the emotions wash over her. 'She loved you both so much. She'd take you for long walks, tell you all about the flowers and trees. She said as long as you were connected to nature, you were connected to all Wolfbloods. Even the ones who had died.'

As Jana spoke, Matei began to cry, silent, fierce sobs wracking his body. Jana reached out and pulled him to her, wrapping her arms around him and holding him tight as he finally let out his grief.

*   *   *

41

Emilia chased after TJ, her own happiness making her oblivious to her brother's tears. *It feels so good just to run*, she thought, as the two Wolfbloods crashed through a small coppice of trees and out the other side. *This is where we should always be, outside and completely free –*

TJ skidded to a halt so suddenly that Emilia almost slid into him.

Imara Cipriani was standing right in front of them, her arms crossed and her jaw set in a hard line.

'Mum,' TJ gasped, out of breath. 'How did you –'

'You think I can't find my own cub?' she asked, her low voice dangerously calm.

There was a rustle behind them. Jana and Matei appeared. Jana immediately stepped in front of Emilia and TJ, raising her chin as Imara glowered at her.

'I take responsibility for this,' Jana said firmly.

Imara just shook her head in disgust.

'*Responsibility?*' she repeated angrily. 'You're all over the internet. *Again.*'

'We found a witness to the fire,' Matei began to explain, but Imara cut him off.

'That is no excuse to run wild in the streets on a full moon!'

'Why shouldn't we?' Emilia demanded. 'People only think we're escaped wolves. They aren't looking for Wolfbloods! Being a wolf is the best thing in the world. It's who we are. You can't stop us.'

Imara looked at her steadily. For a moment it seemed as if she wouldn't say anything else at all. Then she spoke, very calmly.

'You're right,' she said.

The four Wolfbloods looked at each other, relieved. But Imara hadn't finished.

'Your foster parents are waiting to say goodbye,' she went on, looking between Matei and Emilia with cold eyes. 'You have relatives in Romania, don't you? They live a long way from the city, so I hear. You can do all the wolfing out you like there.'

Emilia gasped in horror and burst into tears.

Matei put his arms around his sobbing sister, glaring defiantly at Imara. 'We've got a life *here*.'

'Jana,' TJ begged, 'say something!'

'There's nothing she can say,' said his mother. 'She knows I'm right.'

Jana and Imara stared at each other. For a moment, there was complete silence. And then:

'Run,' Jana said.

Matei hesitated. 'What?'

'All her staff are in Norway,' said Jana, still holding Imara's gaze. 'She can't stop you on her own. Run. NOW!'

Matei and Emilia fled. Imara made as if to grab Emilia, but Jana stepped into her path, blocking her way.

Imara curled her lip, growling. 'I thought you were smarter than this.'

'It's the right thing to do,' Jana told her. 'The secret exists to keep Wolfbloods safe. Not the other way round. If you can't see that, then I can't be part of Segolia any more.'

Imara shook her head. 'Let me know where to send your things from *my* house,' she said curtly. 'TJ, let's go.'

'Mum,' TJ said, in a shocked voice. 'She's part of our family.'

Imara threw Jana a hard look. 'Not any more.' She stalked away. TJ went after her.

'Mum,' Jana heard TJ begging, as he followed his mother. 'What's she going to do? Where's she going to go?'

Jana let them go. She knew she'd done the right thing, whatever it meant for her personally. It wasn't as if it was the first time she'd been without a proper home in her life.

She'd been born wild, after all.

Matei and Emilia, on the other hand, needed her help. They'd never slept rough in their lives – she knew they wouldn't have a clue what to do. Besides, if she didn't find them somewhere to hide, Imara would send Segolia's betas after them as soon as they returned from Norway.

Jana sniffed, picking up Matei's scent easily. They had fled south, back towards the city, perhaps thinking that they could lose themselves amid the crowds of humans there. She followed, stopping every now and then to check that Imara wasn't trying to follow her, but of either Segolia's alpha or TJ there was no sign.

Jana began to track Matei and Emilia. It wasn't so

hard. She found them in a damp, derelict house just a couple of miles away from the park.

'If I found you, so can Segolia,' she told them both. 'But I know a good place you can stay. A secret place. An old Wolfblood den I found when I moved to the city. It's warm and cosy and totally safe.'

'We can't hide forever,' Matei pointed out.

'You won't have to,' Jana told him. 'Segolia will decide it's not worth pursuing you any more. You'll be back in your own beds by the weekend. Trust me.'

Matei nodded. 'So where's this den, then?'

Five

Jana and Katrina sat at a table in the Kafe. It was gone closing time, and they were counting out their tips as Alistair, Katrina's dad, went through the receipts for the day. *It's strange how things turn out,* Jana thought. Given how she and Katrina had started off back at Bradlington High, she'd really never expected them to become friends. And now, here Jana was, sharing a flat with her, not to mention working by her side in the Kafe. Katrina hadn't got on with the student that Alistair had found to replace Kay when she'd left, so when Imara threw Jana out . . . well, things just fell into place.

Jana was surprised to find that she quite liked living with Katrina. Besides, working at the Kafe had certain advantages . . .

'Is someone giving out freebies?' Alistair asked, with a frown. 'We're missing six chicken schnitzelburgers.'

Jana grimaced. 'Sorry,' she said. 'I must have forgotten to charge someone. I'll cover it.' She went to pass her tips over to pay for the food, but Katrina beat her to it.

'No way. My trainee, my responsibility,' Katrina declared. 'You can take it out of my tips, Dad.'

'Don't worry about it this time,' said Alistair, smiling at them. 'You're both honest, that's what matters. I'd better be off. Katrina, don't forget that hob still needs a clean, eh?'

'I'll do it in a minute,' Katrina promised, following her dad to the door so that she could lock it behind him. But as she turned the Kafe's 'open' sign over to 'closed', TJ appeared, staring hopefully through the glass.

'We're closed, TJ,' Katrina pointed out.

'I'll just be a minute,' he promised.

'It's all right,' Jana said with a faint smile. She'd hardly seen TJ since Imara had thrown her out of their house.

Katrina let TJ in and closed the door behind him before heading for the kitchen. TJ slid into the booth where Jana was sitting and waited until Katrina was out of earshot.

'Matei and Emilia's foster parents came round to our house again,' he said quietly.

Jana sighed. 'Did your mum change her mind?'

TJ shook his head. 'She wants them sent to Romania, end of. Do you know where they are?'

'No.' It was a lie, and Jana couldn't look him in the eye as she said it. But it was for TJ's own good.

'Mum's not going to stop looking until she finds them,' he warned her.

Jana nodded, biting her lip. She got to her feet. 'I

should get back to work, TJ . . . Thanks for letting me know.'

'Hey,' said her friend, with a grin. 'You and me are a team.'

He held up his fist, clenched so she would bump it. Jana did, feeling even guiltier. But what else could she do? She watched TJ go, then picked up her backpack and called to Katrina, 'I'm going to the shop. Want anything?'

'Nah,' Katrina called back over the sound of furious scrubbing. 'Thanks, though!'

Jana headed out of the door, pausing to sniff the air. There was no sign of TJ. No sign of anyone else, either. She started running, away into the night.

TJ had been waiting on the low, flat roof of one of the neighbouring buildings. As soon as Jana started to run, he dropped down and followed. He knew Jana had been lying when she'd said she didn't know where Matei and Emilia were. He wasn't angry, not really – he got that she was trying to protect him. But he wanted to help Matei and Emilia just as much as she did. He couldn't help them if he didn't know where they were, could he? So tonight, he was determined to find out.

TJ knew he wasn't as good at all this wild Wolfblood stuff as Jana, but despite her teasing over his absence from her lessons, he had actually been paying attention.

He tracked her over the High Bridge and down into the alleyways that threaded around the banks of the Tyne. Jana turned north, heading along the estuary and towards the edge of the city at wolf speed. TJ stayed with her all the way along a deserted path not far from the water, right past an industrial estate with plenty of hidden corners. He thought he'd cracked it – this would be the perfect place for Matei and Emilia to hide . . . but then he realised that ahead of him, Jana had sped up. He tried to follow, but the road divided into two . . .

TJ stopped at the fork. If he didn't work out what way she'd gone soon, Jana's scent would dissipate and he'd lose her completely. But it seemed to go in two directions at once, as if she'd been careful to double back on herself. He carried on searching for several minutes, but it was no good – the trail had gone cold. TJ let out a frustrated sigh. Then he gave up and headed home.

He didn't see the woman sitting in the car, filming him on her phone.

Jana made her way across a car park and ducked under a broken fence, crawling through thick undergrowth to emerge on to a stretch of grassy wasteland that ran beside the river. The landing stages on the opposite riverbank were still in use, but on this side they had been abandoned. Nature had reclaimed the old industrial concrete bunkers that would once have held cargo before loading.

Bushes had grown in to hide them from view so they had become just part of the riverbank. Jana ran across the uneven grass to an arch of old corrugated iron covered by a rusting grille. Glancing around her, she pulled back the grille and slipped beneath it.

To anyone wandering past, the arch would have looked like nothing worth exploring – just an abandoned piece of junk lying flat on the ground. But inside, there was a hidden chute that led underground. Jana slid down the sloped metal tunnel, trying to make as little noise as possible. Once at the bottom she pulled out three fluorescent flares and threw them into the gloom ahead of her to light her way. Further in, the corridor opened out.

A flashlight glared in her face, blinding her.

'You took your time,' said Matei, lowering the torch as Jana blinked.

Behind him, Emilia lit a paraffin lamp. Jana was shocked to see how comfortable the girl was around the naked flame. It was almost unheard of for a Wolfblood to have no fear of fire, let alone one so badly scarred by an inferno. Emilia saw her expression and smiled a little.

'Fire doesn't only burn,' she said softly.

Jana opened her rucksack and produced two chicken burgers. Matei and Emilia began to eat hungrily, obviously starving.

'TJ tried to follow me,' she told them.

'Why don't you tell him we're here?' Matei asked.

'Because I don't want him to have to choose between you and his mum.' She took a breath, dreading what she had to tell them next. 'Guys, look. I'm sorry . . . But Imara is not going to let you go back to your foster parents.'

They both stopped eating and stared up at her, the worry clear on their faces. 'You *said* she'd change her mind,' Emilia reminded her.

'I'm sorry. I thought she would.'

'Then what do we do?' Matei asked. 'We can't stay underground here forever!'

Jana had thought about this and she had a plan. 'I have friends in Stoneybridge,' she explained. 'Ceri and Gerwyn. They're Wolfbloods. They can hide you. It'll just be until we figure out what to do next.'

The two fugitives didn't look convinced. 'Can we wolf out there?' Emilia asked.

Jana nodded. 'Easier than you can here.'

'It's not a home. We need a proper home,' Matei pointed out. 'Not just a temporary one.'

'We'll find one,' Jana promised. 'Look, I can't spring you on Ceri and Gerwyn in the middle of the night, so get some sleep. I'll come back at first light.'

Jana was fast asleep when the noise woke her – a bang and clatter from downstairs that had her on her feet in an instant. She crept to her door and opened it. Katrina was peering out from her room across the corridor. She might have looked scared, but Jana couldn't tell thanks to the gloopy green facemask she'd plastered all over her face.

'Did you lock the door?' Katrina whispered nervously.

Jana kicked herself. She wasn't sure that she had. Katrina pulled out her phone and dialled 999 as Jana crept downstairs.

'Police,' Katrina said into the phone as she followed Jana. Then put her hand over the receiver. 'Jana? Should we order some firemen as well?'

Jana didn't answer. She could smell something . . . a scent that seemed familiar . . .

She reached the bottom of the stairs with Katrina right behind her. Flinging open the door to the Kafe, they saw a dark figure. Katrina screamed, but Jana broke out in a wide smile.

It was Aran!

'It's all right,' she told her flatmate as she pulled her old wild pack-mate into a tight hug. 'He's a friend!'

Katrina looked at the phone in her hand and then put it back to her ear. 'Er . . . sorry,' she said. 'False alarm . . .'

Aran held on to Jana fiercely, only letting go when she started to pull away. 'Aran,' Jana said, looking up at him, 'what are you doing here?'

Aran gripped her hand and pointed to a small figure

slumped in one of the Kafe's booths. 'She can't breathe,' he said, his face tight with worry. 'We need your help . . .'

'Meinir!' Jana exclaimed, running to her side.

Katrina took one look at Aran's sister's pale face and rapid breathing and lifted her phone again. 'I'll call an ambulance.'

'NO!' said Jana and Aran together.

'She just needs rest, that's all,' Jana added quickly, at Katrina's startled look. 'Let's get her upstairs. She can go in my bed. OK?'

Between them they got Meinir upstairs and into Jana's room. Katrina fussed around, wanting to help, but Jana was desperate to speak to Aran alone. Was this because of what Alexander Kincaid had done? He'd used his evil serum to take Meinir's wolf from her – was this sickness from him, too?

'It's OK, Katrina,' she said eventually. 'We can look after her from here.'

Katrina looked anxious. 'Are you sure?'

'Yeah. You go to bed.'

Katrina nodded and backed out of the room.

Aran frowned as Katrina closed the door. 'Why was she so . . . green?'

Jana tried to smile. 'It's called a facemask. It's . . . a girl thing. What's wrong with Meinir?'

Aran shook his head. 'She was so happy when the pack got back to the wild, but then it was as if the forest

53

was making her sick. Alric told me to bring her here. He said you would know what to do.'

Jana thought for a moment and then reached for her phone. She knew exactly who to call.

Six

Dawn broke over the city, grey and damp. The pale sun, when it started to rise, found Matei and Emilia sitting side by side outside Jana's secret den, waiting for her – but she didn't come.

'Where is she?' Matei said eventually, unable to hide his worry any longer. She couldn't have forgotten them, surely?

'Maybe something happened?' Emilia suggested anxiously. 'What do we do?'

Matei wasn't sure. All he knew was that they couldn't hang around the city. But where could they go? Jana had told them about her life in Stoneybridge, but he had no clue where it was or how long it would take them to get there on foot. And anyway, Jana's friends – Ceri and Gerwyn – had no idea who they were. He couldn't just turn up on their doorstep with Emilia and expect their help without Jana to introduce them. They weren't part of the Stoneybridge pack. They hadn't been part of any pack since their parents had died . . .

Matei glanced at his sister's worried face and swallowed hard. He couldn't go to pieces. It was his job to look after her.

He stood up and held out his hand to Emilia. 'Come on,' Matei said. 'We can't just sit around here. I know where we can go.'

Jana, meanwhile, was still in her bedroom at the Kafe, watching as Doctor Rebecca Whitewood carefully checked Meinir over. The Segolia scientist had been the first person Jana had thought of when Aran had asked her to find help for Meinir. An old friend of Mr Jeffries, one of Jana's former teachers at Bradlington High, Becca Whitewood had gone out of her way to help the Wolfbloods affected by Kincaid's awful serum. Jana had got to know her a little better since her move to Newcastle, and was now beginning to think of her as a friend. Not quite enough of one to call the older woman by her first name yet, the way Shannon Kelly did . . . but maybe one day.

'She's displaying all the symptoms of pneumonia,' said Whitewood.

Aran had no idea what she was talking about. 'What's pneumonia?'

'A respiratory infection – a sickness in her lungs.'

Jana shifted anxiously. 'Will she be OK?'

'Your wolf cells strengthen your immune system,' Doctor Whitewood explained, her face calm but concerned. 'Kincaid's serum destroyed Meinir's. I can stabilise her, but we need to get her to Segolia.'

Jana looked at Aran. Neither of them liked that idea.

But what else could they do? 'Then do it,' she said.

'You need to see Imara first,' Whitewood told her.

Jana frowned. 'Why?'

'Because she wants to see you.' Becca sighed. 'I'm sorry, Jana, but I had to tell her I was coming here.'

'Who is Imara?' Aran asked, confused.

'Segolia's new alpha,' Jana told him, and then added, 'and not exactly my biggest fan.'

Jana bit her lip. She didn't want to see Imara. They had nothing to say to each other. Jana had tried working alongside Segolia but that was over now. Better they just went their separate ways, especially with Imara still looking for Matei and Emilia. But then Meinir moaned weakly, and Jana knew she didn't have a choice.

She had to do as Imara wanted.

Jana would have preferred neutral territory for her meeting with Segolia's alpha, but instead Becca drove her to Imara's home. It was a large sandstone house with its own gates and a wide pebble driveway that crunched under foot as they walked from the car to the front door.

Imara let them both in without a word, leading them into the kitchen. There was no sign of TJ – it was early, so he was probably still fast asleep. Imara, stony-faced and silent, sat at one end of the table and gestured for Jana to sit at the other, as if Jana were in a police cell and about to be interrogated. Despite herself, Jana felt her shoulders tensing. She hated being off-balance. This was Imara's territory. She had the upper hand here.

Doctor Whitewood didn't sit. She stood at the kitchen counter instead, nervously fiddling with the handle of a small teacup.

'I'm sorry your friend is so unwell,' Imara began. 'What happened to her was . . . truly barbaric.' She looked over at Becca. 'Tell me what you need.'

'The big lab,' the scientist said immediately. 'Also, haematology should be put on standby.'

Imara nodded 'I will have that arranged.'

Jana was relieved. Perhaps this wasn't going to be as difficult as she'd feared.

But Imara continued to stare at her. She didn't blink, not once, her expression as cold as ice. Jana felt her heart begin to beat faster. Something wasn't right . . .

'But first,' Imara said softly, 'Matei and Emilia . . . You know where they are.'

Jana blinked. 'No. I don't.'

'You can't protect them by lying.'

'I'm not.'

'They'll be safe in Romania,' Imara said. 'With their family.'

'The family they want is here,' Jana exclaimed.

'It's not about what they want,' Imara snapped loudly, making Jana jump. 'You letting them loose has put them and us in serious danger.'

58

'Matei and Emilia aren't dangerous!' Jana said, her voice rising too.

'They have no control,' Imara pointed out, growing angrier still. 'Humans have already seen wolves running wild on the streets. *That's* dangerous.'

Jana set her jaw hard. She had no intention of listening to this!

Imara raised an eyebrow. 'If you want me to help Meinir,' she said, 'help *me* to help Matei and Emilia.'

Jana's heart thundered in her chest. Was Imara really saying what she thought she was? Would she really only help Meinir if Jana gave her Matei and Emilia?

She stared at Imara. The Segolia alpha stared back, impassive and resolute.

Jana thought of Meinir, lying in her bed even now, struggling to breathe as if every breath might be her last. Then she thought of Matei, how he had cried in her arms as she'd told him how much his mother had loved both him and his sister. How could she ever choose between them? She couldn't give up Matei and Emilia – she just couldn't. But she also couldn't let Meinir suffer and die. What was she supposed to do?

Jana's eyes blurred with tears.

'Let me . . . let me take them someplace else,' she begged, trying not to let the tears fall. 'Close to home. Don't send them away. Please.'

Imara raised an eyebrow, utterly unmoved by Jana's

struggle. 'How can you take them anywhere if you don't know where they are?'

Jana let out a single, strangled sob.

'Bring them to me and Doctor Whitewood can take Meinir to Segolia.'

Jana let the tears fall. She was trapped. Eventually she nodded. 'Where?' she whispered.

'Where we all last met . . . where you told them to run. Meet me there at eight o'clock. You have two hours, Jana.' Imara gave her a sympathetic look. 'One day you'll understand why this had to be done.'

It wasn't until they left the kitchen that they all realised TJ had been sitting on the stairs, listening. He looked as anguished as Jana felt, but she didn't speak to him. She couldn't. She fled out of the door, her feet crunching on the pebble driveway.

'Jana!' she heard Becca call after her. 'I'm so sorry!'

Jana didn't stop. She couldn't risk the tears and pain of what she had to do overwhelming her completely. Instead she ran through the dawn at wolf speed, all the way to the secret den. She was about to betray two of her friends, Wolfbloods who had already lost so much in their lives. Jana thought she had felt heartbreak before, but this was a hundred times worse. The thought of Matei looking at her with those dark eyes of his as he realised what she had done . . .

Outside the den she stopped. Jana put her hands over

her face and took deep, shuddering breaths to calm herself.

But Matei and Emilia had gone.

Jana looked around the empty den, trying not to panic. She scrambled out again, scanning the riverbank.

'Matei!' she shouted. 'Emilia?'

Her phone rang in her pocket. She pulled it out, seeing that it was Katrina.

'Yeah?' she said, answering it.

'Er – where are you?' Katrina's voice asked. 'Some more of your friends are here. Apparently you're meeting them?'

Jana froze. 'What friends?'

'That girl and her fit brother,' said Katrina. 'Anyway, I told them you'd be back in a bit because you know . . . work, but –'

Jana hung up and started running before Katrina had even finished her sentence.

Matei, Aran and Emilia were all in Jana's room, sitting with Meinir. Emilia had been instantly fascinated by the pale woman in Jana's bed, and Meinir was just as enthralled by the burned cub. She lifted a weak hand and pushed Emilia's fair hair away from her scars.

'In the wild, that is a mark of honour,' the former Wolfblood told her. 'You are a *tân cerddwr*.'

'A what?'

'A "fire walker". Our pack has a legend. Thousands

of years ago, a powerful Wolfblood, who mastered her fear of –'

'Morning!' Katrina bustled in, completely disrupting the moment. She stopped dead and wrinkled her nose. 'Wow, it's . . . dusty . . . in here. I'll just . . . open a window, shall I?'

She went to the window and pushed it open before turning with another bright smile. 'Jana's on her way. In the meantime, does anyone need anything? An aspirin, or . . .' Katrina looked sideways at Aran, '. . . a shower?'

Aran stared at her blankly. He had no idea what a shower was.

'No, thank you,' said Matei, finally breaking the silence.

'OK,' said Katrina. 'Well then. I'll just be . . . downstairs . . .' She sidled out, shutting the door behind her.

Emilia was still thinking about what Meinir had said. 'But would they stare at me?' she asked. 'In the wild?'

'They would envy you, *tân cerddwr*,' Meinir told the girl gently.

Emilia smiled.

Jana reached the Kafe just as Katrina was preparing to open for the day. Jana was supposed to be working too, but she had other things to worry about first.

'Where are they?' she asked.

'Upstairs,' her flatmate told her. 'Jana – *why* do all of your friends smell like bins?'

62

Jana didn't answer – she was already halfway up the stairs. She found them all in her bedroom, sitting on the edge of Meinir's bed as Emilia listened with rapt attention to her stories about the wild.

'Guys,' she said, looking at Matei and Emilia, 'I'm so sorry I didn't come for you.'

'It's all right,' Matei said. 'Aran told us what happened.'

'Is Segolia coming?' Aran asked.

'Not for a couple of hours. They need time to get things ready.' Jana looked at Matei and Emilia. She really needed to break the news to them, but she just couldn't bring herself . . .

'We'd better get back to the den,' said Matei, getting up and nudging Emilia.

'I want to stay here!' Emilia protested, looking at Meinir.

'Imara will catch our scent,' Matei told his sister.

Jana bit her lip. 'Matei, Emilia,' she began, 'I –'

'It's all right,' Matei smiled. 'We won't need your friends now. Once Meinir's better, we're going to the wild.'

Jana was shocked. 'What?'

'Imara won't find them there,' Aran pointed out. 'They will be safe.'

Jana's phone started to ring as she tried to find something to say. It was TJ, and she went into Katrina's bedroom to answer it.

'Have you told them yet?' he asked immediately.

'No,' said Jana, a feeling of helplessness washing over her again.

'Well, don't. Don't say anything, all right? I'm on my way.'

'Hang on,' said Jana. 'Wait –' But he'd already hung up.

She turned to find that Aran had followed her. 'What is going on?' he asked. 'I know when you're hiding something. You can tell me, Jana.'

Suddenly the weight of it all was too much to deal with alone. Jana closed the door. Then she told Aran everything.

'I feel like I'm betraying them,' she said, when she was done. Jana could feel the tears threatening behind her eyes. Aran pulled her into a hug.

'Imara is threatening Meinir so that you'll surrender those cubs,' he told her. 'Hers is the betrayal. You have no choice. Matei and Emilia will understand that.'

She pulled away and wiped her eyes. 'I won't be able to forgive myself. I'll *never* forgive Imara.'

Aran was silent for a moment. 'Before we left, Alric, our healer Madoc and I made an agreement,' he confessed, the words obviously painful for him. 'Once Meinir is recovered, she will remain here. I am not to bring her back to the wild. She is human now. The wild . . . is a *threat* to her. But she'd never have come to you for help with me if she'd known that. So . . . so I haven't told her.'

Jana took his hand as Aran struggled to hold back guilty tears. She understood. They were in similar positions.

'She'll need Segolia's help. So will you,' Aran pointed out. 'You cannot be their enemy. We can tell Matei and Emilia together.'

Jana nodded with a faint smile. She was so glad he was here.

She opened the door and then stopped dead. Matei and Emilia were right outside. The angry look on Matei's face told her they'd heard everything.

'Matei –' Jana began, but he grabbed his sister's hand and made for the stairs. 'Wait!' Jana called.

It was TJ who stopped them, blocking their way as he came up the stairs.

'Jana,' said TJ, 'you can't do this to them. You can't take them to Imara.'

'We can't let Meinir die!' shouted Aran, his temper rising.

'No one's saying you should!' TJ yelled back.

'TJ,' Jana said. 'If I go against your mum again, Meinir will pay the price.'

Emilia pulled herself away from Matei. 'Then you can't! I won't let Meinir die for us!'

'Look, just listen to me!' TJ shouted, exasperated. 'This isn't about you and Matei, *or* Meinir! It's about Jana.' He looked at her. 'This is about *you* and my mum. She's doing all this to make a point.'

Jana frowned. 'Me?'

65

'Why else would she make you bring them to the same place that you told them to run from before?'

'This doesn't change anything!' said Aran. 'Jana, he's trying to influence you!'

'Yeah?' TJ challenged. 'And what are *you* trying to do?'

Aran snarled, but TJ wasn't going to back down. Angry, the two Wolfbloods went for each other, Aran's eyes yellowing as they butted heads, snarling.

'Aran!'

The voice was weak and came from Meinir, who had forced herself out of bed and staggered into the hallway.

'I will not be an axe over their necks,' she said, her voice faint but firm. 'If there is a choice to make, I will make it. I choose to die. I'd rather leave this world like a Wolfblood than live in it like a coward.' She looked at her brother. 'You would do the same.'

'You can't do this for us,' Emilia said, tearfully, as they helped Meinir back to bed. 'We can go to Romania.'

Meinir gave the girl a weak smile, brushing the hair back from her scar. 'No,' she said. 'You're part of the pack now. Your home is here.'

Something about Meinir's words gave Jana an idea. '*Brwydr* . . .' she muttered.

'Er – what?' said TJ.

'Imara's protecting her pack. I'm protecting ours . . . Stay here, TJ.'

'Wait,' TJ said. 'You're going to meet her?'

But Jana had gone.

Jana ran all the way to the high, wind-swept ruins outside the city where all of this had started. Imara was already there, but this time she had brought three of Segolia's security team, just returned from Norway. One of them growled a warning at Jana as she passed, but Jana ignored her.

'Where are they?' demanded Imara, as Jana circled her.

'Safe,' Jana told her, teeth bared to show her strength. 'Meinir doesn't want your help. Not at this cost.'

'That's honourable,' Imara observed.

'She made her choice,' Jana said. 'I made mine.'

Imara made an annoyed sound in her throat. 'It wasn't a choice. I'm the alpha here, Jana.'

Jana stepped forward, making it clear that she had no intention of backing down. 'I am an alpha too. And Matei and Emilia are my pack. They are protected. You can't touch them.'

Imara looked as if she was about to say something else when a scent reached them both. Matei and Emilia appeared with TJ close behind them. All three went straight to Jana.

'What is this?' Imara asked, looking at her son.

'Did you think she'd just roll over?' TJ asked, standing resolute with his chosen pack.

Imara lunged at Jana, angry and snarling as her eyes yellowed. 'I won't let you turn him against me!'

'I don't need to,' Jana pointed out.

Imara snarled again. 'Take the cubs,' she ordered her people. '*Take them!*'

'Back off,' Jana growled, moving to stand in front of the others, her eyes glowing yellow.

Imara stalked forward, but Jana had no intention of backing down. 'If you want me to kneel,' she said, 'you're going to have to make me.'

With a snarl of rage, Imara transformed completely. Jana only just managed to move in time as the wolf leapt at her. Then Jana transformed herself and the two Wolfbloods circled each other, nipping, snapping. Imara backed up, preparing to leap at Jana. Then she lunged, fangs out and ready to tear Jana apart.

'Stop it!' shouted TJ, rushing up. 'Stop –'

He threw himself between his mother and Jana. TJ screamed as Imara's bared fangs sank deep into his arm. Imara let go immediately, backing away as her cub fell to the floor, screaming in pain. A second later she slipped back into human form.

'TJ!' Imara whispered, distraught.

'You bit me!' he said, clutching his arm and writhing in pain.

'I'm taking you to Segolia, right now,' said his mother, frantic.

TJ struggled to his feet. 'Meinir first,' he said, angry. 'And you let Matei and Emilia go back to their foster parents. You stop chasing them – or I'm gone.'

'TJ –' Imara began.

'I swear,' he said, deadly serious. 'If they go, I go.'

Imara looked stricken as her son stared her down. Then something cold and hard flashed into her eyes. 'Jana's made you quite the manipulator.'

'No,' said TJ, still furious. 'I learned that from my mother.'

His mum stared at him for another moment. Then she walked to Jana.

'Your pack, your responsibility,' she said, her voice full of threat. 'This is still my territory. They step out of line once . . . *you* pay.'

Jana growled, baring her teeth. For a moment it seemed as if the two women might fight again. But then Imara turned away.

The Segolia alpha pulled out her phone and dialled. The others watched, wondering what she was going to do. 'Doctor Whitewood?' she said, after a moment. 'Go to the Kafe. You have a patient waiting.'

Everyone – TJ included – breathed a sigh of relief.

Seven

'So you lied to me,' said Meinir weakly. She was upset, staring up at Aran from her bed in the Segolia lab as Jana and Doctor Whitewood looked on. Meinir was still pale, her eyes sunken into dark rings. Her hands shook a little as she clenched her thin fists.

Aran, upset too, tried to explain. 'If you go back to the wild, you will only get sick again –'

'You can't stand to see me human!' Meinir said, heartbroken. 'You'd rather abandon me here!'

'That's not true!' said Aran, as he stroked the hair back from his sister's face. 'Jana, tell her why she has to stay here!'

Doctor Whitewood's phone rang, and she moved away to answer it.

'If Meinir doesn't want to stay, I can't force her to, Aran,' Jana said, pained by the conflict between her two friends.

Becca spoke quietly into her phone before ending the call. 'Imara wants to see you,' she told Jana. 'She's waiting in her office.'

'OK,' Jana sighed, heading out of the lab and knowing

that if she wasn't careful, she'd be late for work. Again. She was supposed to be at the Kafe, and she couldn't let Katrina down, especially not on karaoke night, which was always very busy. So far her flatmate had cut her a lot of slack, even though Jana knew herself that she'd been too unreliable since she took the job. She *had* to make more of an effort. Still, the situation with Imara was delicate and Jana couldn't just ignore her request. The Segolia alpha had patched things up with TJ and she and Jana had also reached an understanding – they were, after all, on the same side. But the truce was an uneasy one.

'What's the emergency?' Jana asked, as she walked into Imara's office.

'We have a hostile Wolfblood,' said the Segolia alpha, standing up from her chair and moving around her desk as Jana came in. 'Mostly she's been preying on livestock but she attacked a farmer last night. I need you to track her down.'

Jana frowned. 'Why me?'

'We lost the trail,' said Imara. 'And right now, you're the only who can find it. If this Wolfblood isn't caught quickly, more people will be hurt and our secret could be exposed.'

'What will you do with this Wolfblood, once you have her?'

'Help her,' Imara said, as if it were obvious. 'Now, will you help *us*?'

They looked at each other stiffly for a moment, two alphas making their positions clear. Then Jana nodded. 'Of course.'

Imara relaxed a little. 'Thank you,' she said, with a smile. 'I can take you to where our team lost her scent.'

Jana resigned herself to being late for work at the Kafe and nodded. As the two women walked out of Segolia together, she asked, 'What do you think made this Wolfblood so aggressive?'

'I don't know. We have good people who can figure that one out.'

Jana thought for a moment, an idea forming in her mind. 'Maybe I can help . . .'

Imara smiled as they reached her car. 'You just tell us where she is – we'll do the rest.'

'I'm not a sniffer dog,' Jana said, a little frostily. 'I thought you wanted my help?'

'I just don't want to put you in any . . . unnecessary danger,' Imara told her.

Imara drove Jana as deep into the woods outside the city as she could. Then she parked in a lay-by where another car waited. As they pulled up, Segolia employees were busily loading tranquilliser guns. Jana grimaced at the sight of them. If she had her way, she'd ban Segolia from using them entirely.

72

They ran into the forest, Imara and Jana leading the small pack. Imara led them to a pond, its water glinting with the sunlight that filtered down through the canopy of leaves ahead. It was a beautiful place – the kind of place Jana would have sought out herself had she still been living in the wild.

'We lost the scent here,' Imara said, slowing to a halt.

Beside the water was a camp, although that was a generous term for it. No one who had stayed here would have been very comfortable – it was just an old green blanket lying amid the dry fallen leaves. Jana crouched and picked it up, sniffing. Beneath the blanket was a black woolly hat, which also bore the scent of a Wolfblood.

Jana pushed one hand into the forest mulch. Her eyes yellowed, her heartbeat quickening as Eolas swallowed her. She followed the scent, racing through the dark, shadowy woods on the overwhelming tide of her wolf senses. Eolas took her to a huddle of rocks. A hooded figure was lurking there, shoulders hunched as Eolas brought Jana closer. It looked up suddenly, right at Jana – an angry face with yellow eyes and a snarling mouth.

Jana jerked out of Eolas. 'That Wolfblood has the morwal!' she gasped, shocked.

'The what?' Imara frowned.

Jana didn't have time to explain. A Wolfblood that had become the morwal was indeed dangerous. Morwals were where the old legends of werewolves had come from – something had hurt this Wolfblood so deeply that her wolf had become vicious and cruel. If she wasn't found and helped, she would carry on attacking anything – any*one* – she could.

'The large rocks on the other side of the woods,' Jana said, still breathless from the shock of what Eolas had shown her. 'Near water. Go – now!'

Imara nodded to the Segolia hunters. One of them took the beanie from Jana, and then they were off. Jana made to follow them, but Imara held her back.

'I can help!' Jana said, frustrated.

'I think Segolia can manage,' Imara said sharply, and then added, 'Please. Trust us.'

Back in the laboratory, Meinir was being driven slowly mad. The beep of the machines, the stark white lighting, the clinical smells . . . it was all just too much. Too *human*.

She pushed herself up, struggling to get off the bed even though her legs were almost too weak to carry her. The movement startled Aran, who had been dozing by her side.

'What are you doing?' he asked, as she stood, swaying slightly.

'What does it look like?' Meinir snapped, trying to get past him. 'I'm not staying here!'

'Doctor Whitewood,' Aran said, following Meinir

across the lab as Becca appeared through the double doors. 'Tell her!'

Doctor Whitewood stood very still for a moment, as if she were debating something with herself. When she spoke, her words were clear and quiet.

'I think I've found a way to bring back your wolf.'

Meinir and Aran both stared at her. That wasn't what either of them had expected to hear.

'We have a serum,' the scientist went on, into their shocked silence. 'It's only in the trial stages, but it could work. We've made modifications to Kincaid's original toxin.'

'He was trying to destroy us!' Meinir rasped, horrified to even hear the man's name. 'Why would you keep his poison?'

'You need the disease to make the cure,' Becca explained gently. 'Look, best-case scenario: it works. You get your wolf back.'

'And the worst case?' Aran asked, still suspicious.

Whitewood shrugged slightly. 'You don't. This is up to you, Meinir. Yes, it's a risk – but if you ever want to live safely in the wild again, this may be your only real chance.'

Meinir looked at Aran and then around the lab. It was cold here, not in temperature but in feeling. The whole place was so white, so . . . unnatural. Meinir didn't want to stay another second. But if doing so meant she could eventually go back to the wild . . . as a real Wolfblood . . .

She nodded weakly.

'Do it,' she whispered.

It took a while for Becca to set up the drip. Then all they could do was wait. Beside the bed, Aran twitched nervously, and the scientist knew he didn't really trust either her or the machinery that surrounded his sister. It made Becca nervous. As did the fact that nothing seemed to be happening to Meinir at all. All the data – not to mention what had happened when Kincaid had taken a similar serum – suggested the effect should be instantaneous.

'You don't feel anything?' she asked.

Meinir shook her head. 'Nothing.'

Doctor Whitewood tried not to make her worry obvious. 'These things can take time,' she said. 'We won't know the full outcome until the next full moon anyway, so we'll keep you under observation until then.'

But Meinir could tell things weren't right. 'Your cure has failed!' she sobbed.

'We don't know that,' Becca soothed.

Meinir turned her head to Aran, her movement jerky and agitated. 'My wolf is *gone*!'

Her brother squeezed her hand, upset too, but what could Aran do to help her? If Doctor Whitewood, with the whole of Segolia and this mighty laboratory couldn't change anything, how could Aran, who knew as little about this human world as she did?

Meinir felt her eyes fill with tears. She couldn't stay here a moment longer. She just couldn't. She pulled herself away from Becca, dragging the drip out of her arm.

'Meinir – don't be foolish,' Aran begged.

'You don't make my decisions,' she said, her voice breaking as she started to run, desperate to get away from all of this. Desperate to get away from herself.

Aran chased after her.

Imara and Jana were still at the makeshift campsite. Jana paced, wanting to be doing something rather than just standing around. She was so tense that she jumped when Imara's phone rang.

'Have they got her?' she asked impatiently, as Imara answered it and listened silently.

Imara hung up. 'That was Doctor Whitewood,' she said. 'Aran and Meinir have left Segolia.'

'What?' Jana burst out. 'Why?'

'I don't know,' said Imara, exasperated. 'Find them! Take them back there or send them to the wild – just get them off the streets!'

Jana set off, cutting through the woods at wolf speed. She wondered what had happened to make the two wild Wolfbloods run. Meinir still wasn't well.

An unfamiliar scent brought her up short. Jana skidded

to a halt, all her senses sparking into high alert. She sniffed, turning slowly, her whole body tense as she tracked the strong scent that told her there was another Wolfblood very close.

The forest was silent. There was no sign of life other than her own stilled breathing. Perhaps she'd been mistaken. Perhaps –

A sudden movement above her snapped her to attention. Jana looked up, just in time to see a figure hurtling towards her.

Then everything went black.

Eight

Jana faded back into consciousness. She groaned as she rolled over, her head aching and foggy. A voice was talking somewhere nearby, but not to her. As her vision cleared, Jana could see the person who had attacked her. Whoever it was seemed to be using Jana's phone.

'TJ, it's Carrie. I need you to call me,' said the voice. 'I'm –'

Jana got to her feet, growling. The figure turned and Jana saw that it was a girl a little younger than she was – a Wolfblood with long hair and dark eyes, her clothing the worse for wear. This must be the 'stray' Segolia was looking for. The girl snarled and they leapt at each other, tussling to the ground and struggling amid the leaves. The girl was strong but Jana was stronger. She managed to flip her attacker on to her back, pinning the other Wolfblood there with her hands over her head.

'Get off me!' her quarry shouted, but Jana wasn't going to move. She wrestled her phone from the girl's hand and looked at the screen.

'TJ?' Jana said, looking at the number the girl had been calling.

She held it to her ear, but there was only the sound of his answerphone message on the other end of the line, not TJ himself.

Jana shook the girl. 'Why were you trying to call TJ?'

'Let me go!' the girl shouted, still struggling.

Jana grabbed her by the shoulders, furious, her head still aching from being knocked unconscious. 'Tell me why!'

A sharp scent drifted through the woods to Jana.

'Segolia's coming,' she hissed. '*Tell me!*'

'Please,' the girl burst out. 'TJ can help me! Please!'

Jana could hear the sound of the Segolia security team coming closer. She had no idea what the girl meant, but if Jana let Imara get to her she'd never find out. She got to her feet, pulling the girl with her.

'TJ's my friend,' she said. 'Come with *me* or go with them. Your choice.'

The girl looked at her suspiciously for another moment. Then she nodded. They ran at Wolfblood speed, until Jana was sure they had left Imara and her people far behind. Slowing to a stop Jana dropped to her knees and placed her hand against the ground, slipping into Eolas to find Meinir and Aran. She traced their mad dash through the city, through unfamiliar roads that must have been terrifying for Wolfbloods who were only used to the wild. Aran had almost been hit by a car and Meinir had dragged him into the calm greenery of a churchyard, but they hadn't stayed there long. Meinir was still weak and they both needed food – Jana reached the end of their route and found them at the doors of a corner shop not far from the Kafe, sniffing out the packs of raw meat. Jana wished she could go and get them herself, but she had to deal with whatever was going on with this girl – she couldn't just leave her to Segolia.

Jana pulled out her phone and called Matei.

'There's no time to explain,' she said, as soon as he answered. 'Aran and Meinir have run off. They're in the city, near the Mini-Mart close to the Kafe. Can you and Emilia get them back to Segolia? I'm busy.'

She waited just long enough to hear Matei say, 'Sure . . .' and then she hung up. Jana turned to find the girl staring at her.

'What did you just do?' she asked. 'That "touching the ground" thing . . .'

'Eolas. It's an ability. It lets me find my pack and other Wolfbloods. It's how I found you.' Jana could see the distrust in her eyes. She stuck out her hand with a smile. 'I'm Jana, by the way.'

The girl looked at Jana's offered hand, but didn't shake it. There was a pause and then she said, 'I'm Carrie.'

'How do you know TJ?' Jana asked.

For a moment it looked as if Carrie wasn't going to answer. Then she sighed and muttered, 'We went to the same school.'

Jana decided not to ask more questions for the moment. She wanted to keep moving. She turned and set off. 'Come on,' she said, over her shoulder. But Carrie didn't move.

'Where are we going?' she asked.

'Somewhere safe,' Jana assured her, sticking her hands in her pockets.

'No,' Carrie said firmly. 'I want to see TJ.'

'You will,' Jana told her. 'Soon.'

'No!' Carrie insisted. 'Now. Call him *now*.'

Jana turned. 'Why?' She walked back towards the girl. 'You've risked your life coming here to find TJ. Why?'

Carrie shrugged, rubbing the toe of her shoe in the leaves. 'Bring him here,' she said. 'You'll find out.'

It was clear there was no way Carrie was going to tell her what was going on without TJ. He was between lessons at school when she called, but she could tell she'd caught his attention when she told him who she was with.

'Carrie? Carrie *Black*?' he said, shocked. 'From school?'

'She wants to see you,' Jana told him.

'Why?' TJ sounded confused.

'I thought you could tell me?'

'Nope. No idea. I've got geography . . .'

'She's in trouble. Your mum's after her. She's been preying on livestock, and she attacked a farmer.' Jana heard TJ sigh, as if this wasn't a surprise, just an annoyance. 'She needs help, TJ. Can you just get to the den?'

82

'OK,' he said. 'OK, I'm coming.'

They hung up and Jana turned to the girl. 'He'll meet us at our den. Come on.'

Jana set off. Carrie hung back for a moment as if reluctant to follow, but then she did. They headed through the forest, the summer sun warm where it shone through the leaves overhead. Jana led Carrie to the hidden den, careful to avoid the Segolia team still searching the woods behind them.

The den was dark, especially after the brightness of the day outside, but Carrie didn't seem to mind. Jana wanted to call Matei to find out what was happening with Aran and Meinir, but she sensed that taking her attention away from Carrie was a bad idea. If the girl decided to run again, anything could happen. Anyway, Jana needed to find out why Carrie had become the morwal if she wanted to find a way to help her.

'Carrie,' she began gently. 'Did your parents ever talk to you about the morwal?'

Carrie wandered to a pile of old sandbags and sat down on them. A thin light filtered from above, casting her face in shadow and making her look even younger than she was. 'What's a morwal?'

Jana sat down too, trying to work out how best to explain. 'Well, when something bad happens to a Wolfblood, all the horrible feelings inside can start to build up. They get into your wolf, make it angry. They make it . . . not you. Kind of like a werewolf.' Carrie gave her an incredulous look, but Jana carried on. 'I think . . . maybe that's what's happened to you.'

Carrie gave a half-laugh and shook her head. 'I've always been like this. My parents – they never even told me what I was until I started changing.'

'You're not born with the morwal, Carrie,' Jana told her. 'It's pain. It's brought on by something. I *know*. And I know talking about it can make it better.'

'I haven't come here to make it better!' Carrie shouted angrily. 'I've come here to *kill* it!'

Jana was shocked. 'What do you mean?'

'Kincaid,' Carrie said. 'He can get it out of me. The wolf. TJ knows where he is. He can take me to him. *That's* why I'm here.'

Jana stared at her, a sliver of cold slipping down her spine at the mention of the man's name. 'Kincaid's gone,' she said.

Carrie shook her head. 'TJ knows where he is. He can take me there. That's why I'm here.'

Jana blinked. What was she talking about? TJ had never even met Kincaid, so how could he know where the scientist was?

Jana's head swam. 'Wait here,' she said, standing up. 'I just need some air. I'll be back.'

She went back up the chute and stood in the afternoon sunlight, turning everything over and over in her head. Segolia had taken Kincaid away somewhere, locked the scientist up for what he'd tried to do to all Wolfbloods. But TJ was Imara's son, and Imara was Segolia's alpha . . . If Segolia had Kincaid somewhere close by then Imara would know, wouldn't she? And perhaps so would TJ . . .

A sound came to her – it was TJ, running across the wasteland towards her. She turned on him, angry.

'What did you tell Carrie about Kincaid?' she demanded.

'What?' TJ said, shocked by her anger. 'I didn't tell her anything!'

'That's why she's here, TJ! She thinks you can take her to him so he can get rid of her wolf!'

TJ shook his head. 'It was just a stupid story,' he protested.

'*What* was?'

TJ made a face. 'I sort of told her at school that I knew him. Knew where he was.' At Jana's look he said, 'She was new, OK? I was trying to – don't get all judgey with me!'

'Great,' said Jana, deeply unimpressed. 'Well, now you have to tell her the truth. If she sees that Kincaid can't help her, then maybe she'll let me. She's the morwal, TJ.'

TJ looked over his shoulder towards the den, worried. 'Jana, you have to give her to Mum,' he said. 'This isn't the same as Matei and Emilia! Segolia can *help* Carrie . . .'

'Imara asked me to track Carrie's scent and I did,' Jana reminded him hotly. 'I'm doing this on my own.'

'Well,' said TJ, with a slow smile as he pointed to his chest. 'Not quite . . .'

Jana thumped him, exasperated. '*You* owe Carrie the truth,' she said. 'And she won't listen to me until you tell her Kincaid and his serum are gone.'

TJ nodded and followed Jana inside the den. Carrie leapt up as they came in, relieved when she saw TJ.

'I need you to take me to Kincaid,' she said, immediately.

'I can't,' TJ told her, awkward and ashamed. 'Carrie . . . Kincaid can't help you. He was sent away somewhere. I don't know how to find him. No one does. I lied. I'm sorry.'

For a second the girl looked devastated. Then something else passed through her eyes – a rage deeper than Jana had ever seen. Carrie screamed and then leapt at TJ. Jana jumped in to push her away and Carrie screamed again as Jana held on to her. Then, suddenly, Carrie burst into tears.

'I'm a monster,' she sobbed helplessly. 'What do I do?'

'Let Jana help,' TJ said. 'You can trust her.'

'Tell me what happened to you,' Jana urged. 'We'll keep your secret, whatever it is. We're good at that.' But Carrie just shook her head.

'Well,' began TJ. 'If you can't tell her, maybe you can

86

show her? Jana can do this thing. Can't you? Ansion. It lets her see the past . . .'

Carrie looked up at Jana through her tears. 'If you see, then you'll understand. It was – it was an *accident* . . .'

TJ gave Jana a beseeching look. Jana took a deep breath and moved closer to Carrie.

'Are you sure about this?' she asked, reaching for the girl's hands.

Carrie nodded. Jana clasped her fingers gently and closed her eyes. Ansion swallowed her whole as Jana's eyes flashed yellow. The crackle of fire engulfed her – Jana could hear the sound of running – Carrie screaming, someone else crying –

'Who's this?'

It was Matei's voice. Jana jolted away from Carrie and turned to see him standing at the other end of the dark den with Emilia, Aran and Meinir.

Carrie completely freaked out. She snarled, lunging past TJ and Jana before they had chance to stop her. Matei shoved Emilia behind him, his eyes yellowing angrily as he bared his teeth, protecting his sister.

'You tricked me!' Carrie screamed at Jana. Then a shudder passed through her and she put her hands up to her face. 'It's . . . happening . . .' she hissed.

Jana held her by the arms. 'Fight it, Carrie,' she ordered. 'You can –'

'LIAR!' Carrie roared, right in Jana's face, trying to claw

herself free of Jana's grip. Jana shoved the girl backwards, trying to subdue her. Aran leapt to help, on the brink of transforming himself, his wolf fangs on full display.

Carrie stumbled and then seemed to regain her old self, just for a second. 'Run,' she begged them all. 'It's coming. RUN!'

'No!' Jana shouted, determined not to leave Carrie to deal with the morwal alone.

Carrie howled, barging past her, eyes fully yellow. She pushed through the gathered Wolfbloods, making for the den entrance, but Meinir was in her way. Carrie threw her, pinning her against the wall as Meinir sobbed, utterly petrified.

For a second it looked as if Carrie would rip Meinir's throat out with her teeth, but then she stumbled backwards, retching. She fled out of the den.

'Go after her!' Aran shouted, running to his sister.

Jana and TJ chased after Carrie, leaving the others to look after Meinir. By the time they got out of the den, Carrie had fully transformed – into a huge wolf with a glossy coat running into the distance. Jana and TJ followed as fast as they could. Jana didn't dare to transform herself – Carrie was heading for the city and there were far too many people about in the middle of the day. She dashed down streets and through gardens, terrifying everyone she came across. Eventually Carrie jumped a stone wall into a series of playing fields. Jana and TJ skidded to a halt as they realised that a whole group of people had pulled out their phones and were filming. They couldn't follow – they'd be caught on camera too. Sure, they were in human form, but someone was sure to ask them what they knew about the wolf if they carried on.

TJ pulled out his own phone and held it to his ear.

'What are you doing?' Jana asked.

TJ looked at her. 'Calling my mum,' he said, flatly. 'Like *you* should have.'

After TJ had explained to Imara what had happened, they went back to the den. Meinir was still in shock, but it wasn't Carrie she was afraid of – it was herself.

'I was scared,' she said, horrified by her own weakness. 'I was like – a *human* . . .'

Aran held his sister, 'Shh,' he soothed, although everyone could see he was just as upset.

'The pack will turn me away . . .' Meinir whispered, sounding utterly devastated. Then suddenly, she cried out. Her body began to convulse, lurching out of Aran's arms as Meinir's limbs stiffened.

'Meinir?' Jana asked, grabbing her hand. 'What is it?'

Meinir couldn't answer. Her whole body was shaking. Aran tried to still her, but couldn't hold on. Something was very, very wrong . . . Meinir wrenched herself away from her brother, scrambling forward on her hands and knees. Then she craned her neck, tipping her head back as black veins bloomed and spread across her face.

'Doctor Whitewood's serum!' Aran shouted, in happy astonishment. 'It's working!'

Meinir's eyes yellowed and she began to laugh. 'She's back!' she cried. 'She's *back*!' She howled out of sheer joy. The rest of the Wolfbloods howled too, as happy as Meinir was herself.

The pack stayed at the den for the rest of the day, watching as Meinir grew stronger and stronger. The Wolfblood regained more of herself with every passing moment, until eventually she grew restless. Meinir was a true wild Wolfblood – she couldn't bear to be in the city for any longer than absolutely necessary. She wanted to go back to the wild. She wanted to go *home*.

They all gathered outside the den to say goodbye. Matei wrapped an arm around his little sister, knowing that she was sad to see Meinir go. There was something about the older Wolfblood and her tales of life in the wild that had completely enchanted Emilia.

Meinir stood in front of Jana, strong, proud and smiling.

Jana smiled back, delighted for her friend. 'You're ready for this,' she said.

'I feel *me* again,' Meinir said, before she clasped Jana's arm and touched her forehead to forehead in the traditional Wolfblood greeting of affection. 'Thank Doctor Whitewood for me?'

Jana nodded and Meinir moved aside, letting Aran take her place. He frowned as he looked at Jana, apparently reluctant to say goodbye. Eventually he touched his forehead to hers and then stood back, his arm still entwined with hers.

'Come with us,' Meinir urged, but Jana shook her head. She couldn't go with them, not now.

Aran still didn't let her go. 'You are adrift, Jana,' he said.

Jana couldn't pretend she wasn't tempted. To run with a real wild pack again – to see her father – how wonderful that would be. But she looked at all of her city friends and knew what she had to do.

'No,' Jana said, quietly. 'I know I have a purpose here. I just need to find it. But I'll miss you.'

Aran looked at her seriously, as if he were trying to read a truth hidden deep in her eyes.

'Both of you,' Jana added, turning to smile at Meinir, too.

'Can *we* come?' Emilia asked hopefully, earning a playful cuff around the ear from her brother.

Meinir went to the girl, brushing Emilia's hair back from her scar gently before giving her a warm smile. 'You're needed here, *tân cerddwr*.' Emilia threw her arms around Meinir, shutting her eyes and holding on as if she never wanted to let go. The wild Wolfblood hugged her back for a long time before pulling away with another smile.

Then they were gone.

Karaoke night at the Kafe was in full swing as Jana walked in. Katrina's dad was serving drinks while Katrina and a visiting Kay were belting out Spice Girl tunes with enough enthusiasm to power the lights at a night game in St James's Park.

'I pay you to work here, Jana,' Katrina's dad Alistair said, evidently not pleased that Jana had missed yet another day of shifts.

Jana felt terribly guilty. How could she explain that things just kept getting in the way? 'And I *want* to be here . . .' she assured him. 'I do.'

'Well,' said Alistair, nodding. 'Katrina swears by you. That's all I need.' He went back to serving the customers.

'Hey,' said TJ, appearing beside her. 'You all right?'

As Jana turned to him a scent came to her, strong and familiar.

Jana whipped her head around as something came crashing through the Kafe's front window, glass breaking into the room. It was Carrie, transformed into her full wolf-self. She was huge, with her hackles up and her fangs bared. Utter pandemonium broke loose. The Kafe filled with the shrieks and screams of terrified customers as they tried to flee, running this way and that. TJ and

Jana dropped to the floor, hiding as Katrina and her dad herded everyone into the kitchen.

'Transform!' TJ whispered to Jana, but she couldn't – Katrina and her dad were peering through the glass window in the kitchen door!

Wolf-Carrie growled as she stalked Jana, trapping her in a corner so that there was no way that Jana could escape. TJ grabbed a chair and rushed at the wolf, but Jana held up her hand to stop him, shaking her head. TJ lowered the chair and watched as Jana kept her hand high, holding it out to the wolf as it approached. If she could just get Wolf-Carrie to trust her . . .

Katrina burst out of the kitchen, the fire extinguisher in her hand. She blasted the wolf in the face, spraying her with foam. The creature howled and backed away, crashing blindly out of the Kafe. Katrina dropped the extinguisher and slammed the door behind it, throwing the bolts.

Jana and TJ raced through the kitchen and out of the back door as the wolf careened down the street and straight into a Segolia tranquilliser dart, fired by one of Imara's people. Carrie crashed, unconscious, to the pavement.

Jana saw Imara watching them from a distance. It was over.

Later, she and TJ went back to Imara's house to try to explain what had happened.

'I was getting through to her,' Jana said, frustrated as

the three of them sat around the table. 'Something scared her off . . .'

Imara shook her head. 'You think only you can solve problems, Jana, but most of the time, you just create more.'

Jana dropped her head, ashamed.

'We will look after her. I promise,' Imara told her. 'We have the people and the resources to deal with precisely this sort of thing. Carrie's going to be fine.'

'I know,' said Jana, upset. She'd thought she was doing the right thing – all she'd wanted to do was help Carrie, without her having to end up shut in a room somewhere for goodness knew how long. As far as Jana was concerned, that wouldn't be any better than being in a cage.

'Come on,' protested TJ, seeing how distressed Jana was. 'Carrie's got help, Meinir's all fixed and Katrina's a total legend! It's all good!'

Jana wasn't convinced, but Imara smiled at her. 'You ask a lot of yourself, Jana,' she said. 'And rightly – you're a talent. But you can't save the world on your own.'

Imara got up and left them alone. Jana sighed as she looked at TJ.

'She's right, isn't she?' Jana said. 'I just seem to be doing more harm than good these days.'

Frowning, TJ took her hand. 'Hey,' he said. 'Carrie's going to get better and she's going to remember what you did for her. That's good. You come out to bat for *everyone*,

Jana. That's what makes you great. Don't let what happened today change that. Don't let *anything* change that.'

Jana squeezed his hand. 'Thanks, TJ.'

'Hey,' TJ grinned, 'we're a team, right?'

'Yeah,' she smiled back. 'A team.'

Nine

TJ, Emilia and Matei were sitting on a bench in the school gym at Hawthorn Secondary School, part of a crowd that had gathered to watch Selina Khan spar with Hannah. The two girls were rivals at tae kwon do, and TJ would always cheer Selina on if he had the chance. He just thought she was awesome. Pretty cute, too – not that he'd ever tell anyone that . . .

'Come on, Selina!' TJ shouted as she ducked and dived, easily missing all of Hannah's jabs. He turned to his two friends. 'How cool is she though, seriously?'

'Very cool,' agreed Emilia.

Matei shrugged. 'I've seen cooler,' he said. Then he watched as Selina made Hannah back up with a series of expert blows. 'Maybe not,' he admitted.

'Do you think she'd teach me?' Emilia asked eagerly.

'Totally,' said TJ. 'She lives for this stuff!'

The match continued until Selina's belt came undone. 'Break!' she called, turning away to do it up. Hannah pretended not to hear. She kicked out while Selina's guard was down, sweeping Selina's legs from under her so that she ended up flat on the mat.

'That's not fair!' Emilia shouted.

'Oh, come on!' TJ yelled, incensed, as Hannah's cronies cheered. He ran over to see if Selina was all right. As he leant over her, TJ was shocked to see that Selina's eyes were wolf-yellow. She was veining up, too – about to wolf out completely!

He jumped on top of her, holding her down before her wolf could appear. Behind him, a ripple of surprise ran through the crowd, followed by laughter and a whistle or two.

'I don't think she needs mouth-to-mouth, TJ,' Hannah jeered, to more laughter.

'Get off me!' Selina hissed, as TJ pinned her to the floor.

'Look at your hands!' he whispered.

Selina looked but the veins had already disappeared. She pushed TJ away with an angry growl.

'I was trying to help!' he said. Then he saw her face and decided that the best course of action was to run. He fled from the gym, the sound of laughter following him all the way.

He caught up with her later as Selina walked home.

'Selina!' TJ called, but she just walked faster, trying to get away from him. 'I'm sorry. I had to do something,' he said.

'You really embarrassed me,' Selina told him,

stopping briefly and giving him a stare that could pulverise rock.

'I only got involved when you . . .' he dropped his voice to a whisper, '. . . veined up!'

Selina narrowed her eyes. 'When have I ever veined up in front of you – or anyone else?'

'Never,' admitted TJ.

'Thank you!' She walked away.

'Why would I make this up?' TJ asked, walking with her.

Selina looked awkward. 'Do I really need to spell it out?'

TJ realised what she meant. 'Whoa,' he said. 'You think I'm doing this because I fancy you? Not that I'm saying I do, obviously . . .'

'I'm sorry. You're a nice guy, but can we just be friends? Online,' Selina added, with a spiky edge to her voice. 'With filters. From a distance . . .'

'But I – Let me just –'

'Besides, you can't just wolf out and have no clue about it,' Selina went on angrily. 'And I've worked too hard for too long to have you mess up my chances of competing in the regional tournament. I'm going to win that trophy, and nothing and no one is going to stop me. Not you, not Hannah. Right?'

'Right,' TJ said, defeated.

'Thank you,' said Selina, with distinct finality. 'And goodbye.'

She turned her back on him and stalked away, obviously still angry. TJ watched her go, worried.

Later, after he and his mother had made and eaten dinner together, TJ did the washing-up. Imara sat at the kitchen table, working on her laptop as she often did in the evenings. TJ couldn't stop thinking about what had happened with Selina earlier in the day.

'Mum,' TJ began, 'I was wondering about Wolfbloods who vein up in front of people . . .'

Imara instantly looked up with a worried frown. 'What have you done?'

'Me? Nothing! I was just remembering when Jana told us about her arriving in Stoneybridge and how she kept veining up . . . How is it even possible to wolf out without knowing?'

Imara shrugged. 'There could be any number of reasons. Physical or psychological.'

'What would Segolia do if one of us did that here?' he asked.

'If someone was that unstable, we'd take care of them.' His mother gave him a serious look. 'TJ, if you have anything to tell me, now would be the time.'

TJ looked down into the dish water for a moment. 'We need a dishwasher,' he said, at last.

'I've got one,' Imara pointed out. 'And he hasn't finished.'

TJ sighed and carried on scrubbing the pots and pans. When he'd finished he put everything away before going upstairs to finish his homework, but he couldn't concentrate. He tried to stop thinking about Selina, but what had happened kept going around and around his head. She *had* veined up. TJ knew he hadn't imagined it. But if she didn't even know she was doing it, how would he ever be able to work out why it was happening? And if he couldn't work out why, he wouldn't be able to help her stop it – and if it kept happening then Segolia would . . . Well, he didn't know what Segolia would do, not really, but he had an idea that it wouldn't be anything he'd want to see Selina go through. So that was the point where he tried to stop thinking all together but somehow TJ just ended up going right back to the beginning again. Selina was veining up and she didn't even know it. But *why*?

TJ eventually fell asleep and dreamed of an angry wolf with beautiful, shining eyes pacing around the school gym while Hannah and her coven of mates, all in tae kwon do gear, kicked and punched the creature until she cowered in fear.

It wasn't a good dream.

The next morning TJ decided to go and find Jana at the Kafe. She was working, but took a break when he came in.

'I need to talk to you,' he said, in a low voice as they sat down at one of the booths. 'It's about something serious.'

'Is this about what happened with you and Selina?' Jana asked.

'Yeah . . .' said TJ, surprised. 'How do you know?'

Jana gave a smile that turned into a slightly awkward grimace. 'Matei described your romantic moves as . . . kind of a rugby tackle.'

TJ sighed. 'I'm freaking out.'

'You'll get over it,' Jana said, with a shrug. 'There are plenty more wolves in the woods!'

'No!' he stopped her, hurriedly. Why did everyone think he fancied Selina? 'She was fighting and she veined up. The weirdest thing was she didn't even know she'd done it.'

Jana didn't look as if she believed him. 'Really? Has she done it before?'

TJ shook his head. 'No. I've known Selina for years. She's super-straight. She'd never let the wolf out.'

Jana shrugged. 'So what's changed?'

'I don't know, but she's proper fixed on winning this tae kwon do tournament. Can you imagine if she wolfs out in that?' Jana's face told him she was suddenly taking notice. 'It's just . . . she thinks I'm making it up because I fancy her,' he said.

Jana raised her eyebrows. 'Don't you?'

101

'Yes,' he said immediately, then realised what he'd said as Jana grinned. 'No! I mean – look – that's not the issue here!'

Jana relented. 'We'll talk to her after school,' she promised.

But that was easier said than done. As usual, Selina went straight to the gym after lessons, which was where Jana and TJ found her. She was far more interested in teaching Emilia the basics of tae kwon do than she was in talking, though.

'What's going on?' TJ asked, seeing Emilia on the mat as they came in.

'Emilia's decided she wants to learn tae kwon do,' Matei explained, as Selina ignored TJ and Jana completely.

TJ grinned, watching as Emilia kicked the punchbag while Selina held it steady. For a little squirt, the kid wasn't bad.

'Selina,' he said, after a moment, 'can we have a word?'

Selina kept her focus on Emilia. 'How about four?' she suggested. '"I'm. Washing. My. Hair."'

Emilia sniggered, but TJ ignored the jibe and persisted. 'You remember Jana?' he asked. 'She was with me when I came to ask you for Darren's address – she's a friend.'

'Hi,' said Jana, with a friendly smile.

Selina glanced at Jana with a faintly embarrassed look on her face. 'Oh *please* don't.'

Jana frowned. 'What?'

'If this is where a friend who happens to be a girl comes in to tell me what a great guy TJ is . . .'

'Er, no,' said Jana, crossing her arms. 'It's about what happened yesterday. When you veined up.'

'How many times do I need to say it?' Selina said. angrily. 'I didn't vein up! He's making it up!' She turned her attention to Emilia again, moving the younger girl out of the way. 'Emilia, it's very important that you pivot. From. The. Hip . . .'

Selina punctuated each word with a sharp kick to the punchbag. They became harder and harder as Emilia tried to hold it steady for her under the onslaught. Then Selina stopped kicking and started punching instead. As her sudden fury grew, her eyes yellowed and black veins sparked along her arm, clear enough for them all to see.

'Whoa!' said Emilia, her eyes wide and round.

Selina stepped back from the bag and stared at her hands in shock.

'I tried to tell you,' said TJ.

Selina glared at him. 'This is because *you* are stressing me out!' she shouted.

'Selina, listen,' Jana tried.

'Back off!' the girl yelled, pushing past her and heading for the changing room.

Jana shook her head and followed. She found Selina sitting on one of the benches, removing her hand wraps with a worried look on her face. She turned away as Jana sat beside her.

'It used to happen to me,' Jana told her quietly. 'One remark about my clothes and I'd lose it.'

'It's only happening now because of TJ,' Selina insisted, but her voice was quieter.

'Maybe,' Jana agreed. 'Or something else is worrying you. Is there anything going on at home?'

Selina glanced away. 'No,' she said softly, though to Jana's sharp ears she didn't sound too sure about it.

Jana took a wild guess and asked, 'What do your parents think about you doing tae kwon do?'

'They don't –' Selina began, and then stopped herself. 'This is nothing to do with them.'

Jana frowned slightly, a sudden suspicion surfacing in her mind.

'They know you do it, though?'

Selina said nothing for a second, and then went to get up. 'I've got to go . . .'

'Wait,' Jana said, resting a hand on the girl's arm. Even if Selina wasn't prepared to trust her yet, perhaps there was something Jana could do to help her. 'Hold up. Let me show you what someone taught me. You've got nothing to lose, have you?' she said, with an encouraging smile. 'Come on.'

Selina relented and followed Jana back out to the gym. Jana led her to the mat and stood beside the punchbag.

'To stop the wolf you need to recognise it,' Jana explained. 'It's a tingling that spreads across your skin. Go.'

Selina looked unsure, but began to punch at the bag.

'Now imagine the bag is Hannah. She's goading you,' Jana said, imitating what Hannah might say as she gestured for the others to do the same. '"You'll never win, Selina!"'

'Can't you do any better?' Matei taunted.

'Call that a punch?' TJ added loudly.

Selina hit the bag harder and harder, and the Wolfblood began to blacken in her veins.

'Now stop!' Jana grabbed the punchbag, moving it away so that Selina faltered and stumbled. 'Can you feel the tingling?'

Selina's veins subsided, but she was still angry. 'How am I supposed to stop mid-fight? My opponent won't!'

'We're looking for the signs so you can stop it before it gets to that,' Jana pointed out.

Selina threw up her hands. 'Tingling? It's kids' stuff! What you did won't help me.'

'Please,' said TJ. 'Just give it a chance.'

'You have no choice,' Jana told Selina. 'If you don't beat this thing then you'll have to withdraw from the tournament and stop doing tae kwon do altogether. You can't risk veining up in front of humans.'

Selina looked stunned and upset. 'No one asked you to get involved. I'm not giving up! You can't make me!'

She turned and ran from the gym.

'Wait!' TJ called. 'Selina –' He went to run after her, but Jana stopped him.

'Leave it,' she said. 'She's too worked up right now.'

TJ watched Selina go, feeling terrible for her and wishing there was something he could do to help. Unfortunately for TJ, it was a case of 'be careful what you wish for', because Jana's solution was for him to go and talk to Selina's parents.

'I'm pretty sure her parents don't know she's doing tae kwon do,' Jana explained, convinced that the key to Selina's uncontrollable wolfing out was a problem at home.

'Why?' TJ asked, frowning.

Jana shook her head. 'I don't know. That's why I think you should speak to them.'

'Great,' said TJ, with a sigh, imagining exactly what he was going to have to say. '"Mr and Mrs Khan, you know that lovely too good to be true daughter of yours? Well, she *is* too good to be true. She's secretly kung fu-ing up the place behind your back and wolfing out in public, threatening the Wolfblood secret." They are going to *love* me – and so is she! Thanks a lot!'

'You're her friend,' Jana pointed out.

TJ frowned. 'I'm not so sure she'd agree. I'm going to be known forever as Big Mouth Cipriani.'

Jana grinned. 'TJ. You already are.'

106

'Cute, Jana,' he said, pretending to be hurt. 'Really cute . . .'

Selina's mum, Sophia, was glad to see him, though. TJ had gone up and knocked on their door while Jana stood a little way down the road, waiting.

'TJ,' said Mrs Khan, inviting him in with a big smile. 'We haven't seen you for ages. How's your mother?'

'Hello, Mrs Khan,' said TJ, as they stood in the hallway chatting. 'She's fine, thanks. Um, can I have a word? It's about Selina . . .'

'Oh, TJ,' sighed Selina's mum. For some reason she looked a little awkward. 'Look, Mr Khan and I think you're a lovely lad, but I just don't think she thinks of you in that way.'

'Oh – no! No, no!' TJ exclaimed, embarrassed and suddenly relieved that Jana wasn't there. 'It's about something else . . .'

They were interrupted by the sound of Selina bounding down the stairs clutching a red notebook. TJ blinked – here at home, Selina had let her long, wavy dark hair out of the scarf she usually covered it with. She looked even prettier than usual, which took him a bit by surprise, as TJ hadn't thought that was possible. Selina reached the bottom of the stairs before he'd managed to think of anything to say.

'TJ! Have you come about your notes?' Selina waved the red notebook.

He stared at her blankly. 'What?'

Her dark eyes bored into him. 'Your *notes*. I borrowed his notes from the after-school study session,' Selina explained to her mum.

'Did you?' said TJ, mystified. Selina sent him a pleading look.

'Yeah. They were really useful. You are a very smart guy.'

'Yeah, but –' At the look on Selina's face, TJ finally worked out what she was doing and played along. 'Er – oh well, you know it!' he said enthusiastically. 'Study and that – I'm all about the study . . .'

'OK,' said Sophia, smiling again. 'I'll leave you two to it. Nice to see you TJ. Best to your mum.'

As soon as she was gone, Selina turned on him, obviously angry. 'We're meant to be mates!'

'We didn't know what else to do,' TJ whispered back.

'We'll talk about this some other time, right? Right!' TJ sighed as she pushed him towards the door. 'Right.'

'I'll call you later, TJ,' Selina said, louder so that her mum would hear. 'But right now I have an essay to do . . .'

She slammed the door behind him.

'How'd it go?' Jana asked, as TJ reappeared.

'It's . . . sorted,' he lied.

Jana raised an eyebrow. 'How sorted?'

TJ sighed. 'Look – it's done, Jana.'

'Good,' she told him. 'Because your mum's solution would have been a lot worse.'

Jana walked away and TJ had to force himself to catch up. He just hoped he'd bought enough time to figure out what was going on with Selina and help her without dropping either of them in it. TJ had a feeling that if he couldn't do that, they'd both be in big trouble.

The next time TJ spoke to Selina, it was outside school the following morning. He was standing with Emilia and Matei.

'We all wolf out sometimes,' Emilia pointed out.

'Yeah, but we know we're doing it,' said Matei.

Emilia shrugged. 'Wouldn't you wolf out if you had TJ panting after you?' she teased.

Matei made a face. 'If that happens we really are going to Romania . . .'

TJ threw up his hands, exasperated. 'This is not about me! I —' He stopped as they saw Selina approaching.

'Hi, Sel,' Emilia said, with a smile. 'Can we do some more training tonight?'

'Course,' Selina nodded, then looked at TJ. 'Can we talk?'

They walked away from the others.

'If you're going to have a go then get it over with,' said TJ, 'because I was just trying to help —'

'TJ —' Selina tried to break in.

TJ carried on, '– and I didn't think there was any other –'

'TJ!' said Selina. 'Does your mouth ever stop for rest? I wanted to thank you for covering for me.'

TJ blinked. 'It's OK,' he said. 'Sel – why don't your parents know you do tae kwon do?'

'Not this again,' Selina said sharply. 'I'm trying to say thanks.'

'And I'm trying to help.'

'You can help by butting out,' Selina told him. She walked away, but a figure appeared in her path. It was Hannah.

'Spat with the boyfriend?' she taunted.

'He's not my boyfriend,' Selina said. TJ could see her clenching her fist, trying to keep herself calm.

Hannah snorted. 'Don't know why I'm surprised. You don't even have any friends. Let alone a boyfriend.'

Emilia appeared by Selina's side. 'We're her friends,' she said firmly.

Hannah wrinkled her nose as she looked at Emilia's scar. 'I mean friends that you actually want to look at.'

Selina shoved Hannah, and TJ, Matei and Emilia all saw the veins beginning to trace down her neck. The three of them dragged her away.

'That's it,' Hannah called, triumphant. 'Run away with your little friends!'

'Let me go!' Selina said, still struggling.

'Sel – look at your hands!' TJ told her.

She looked down, clearly shocked to see the Wolfblood running through her veins. Selina paled, wrenched herself away and ran.

They found her crouched in a corner of one of the school's quietest rooms, crying. TJ asked Matei and Emilia to give them a moment.

'I could have torn her to pieces,' Selina said tearfully. 'I should've believed you. But tae kwon do is the only thing that's really *mine*. Do you know what I mean?'

'So what are you going to do?' TJ asked.

Selina shrugged, defeated. 'If I carry on, then I'm putting everything at risk . . . *everyone*.' She wiped away her tears and stood up as TJ followed. 'That's not going to happen.'

They went out into the corridor, where Matei and Emilia were waiting. Selina headed for the school notice boards. On one of them was a form titled 'County Tae Kwon Do Tournament'. Selina's name was part of the list. She stood looking at it for a moment, then she took out a pen and scribbled out her name. Hannah appeared behind her, watching with obvious glee.

'Wow,' said Hannah. 'Well – it's for the best. This competition is for people who take the sport seriously, not just amateurs looking for a fight.'

She walked off, flanked by her giggling cronies.

'I'm sorry, Sel,' TJ said quietly.

Selina just nodded and walked away.

Ten

The day after Selina had withdrawn from the tournament, TJ went over to her house after school. He wasn't sure how Selina would react to him turning up at her front door again, but he felt he had to do something. Hopefully the idea that he and Jana had hatched the night before would help a little once Selina knew about it. TJ still hadn't told Jana what had really happened the last time he'd gone to the Khans' house, but fingers crossed now he wouldn't need to. In fact, this should be the answer to all their problems. More than a little nervous, he knocked at the door, smiling as Mrs Khan opened it.

'Hello again, TJ. Come in.'

'Thanks, Mrs Khan,' TJ said, stepping inside. 'Is Selina in?'

There was the sound of footsteps up the path and Mr Khan appeared, heading into the house behind TJ and kissing his wife hello.

'Selina is in, but she's not in the greatest of moods,' said Mrs Khan, as much for her husband's benefit as TJ's.

'Oh?' Mr Khan frowned, looking from Mrs Khan to

113

TJ. 'Anything happen in school that we should know about?'

TJ frowned. 'I think she's just . . . really stressed at the moment,' he said, trying not to sound as if he were hiding something.

At that moment Selina appeared. 'We're going out!' she announced, and then, just to clarify what she meant, added, 'Not like *that*!' She grabbed a headscarf and pushed TJ out of the door, closing it behind them.

They started walking. 'I had to get out of there,' she said, wrapping the scarf over her hair. 'I couldn't face another interrogation about why "Imara's boy" came round. Take me out somewhere.'

TJ gave her a cheeky grin. 'I've got an idea, but you're going to have to trust me.'

Selina looked doubtful, but she followed him as he ran. TJ took her to the hidden den.

'Wow,' Selina said, stepping out of the chute into the dark network of little concrete rooms. 'How old is this place?'

TJ handed her a glow stick before lighting one himself. 'Who knows? Jana found it.'

Selina continued to look around as they walked deeper into the den, 'What are we doing here?'

'Well,' began TJ, taking a deep breath. 'It's a den for us but it's also . . . your new dojo.'

Selina stopped. 'What?'

He smiled, leading the way into one of the larger rooms. 'I figured we can kit it out with everything you need,' TJ explained. 'That way you can practise without stressing out.'

Selina sighed. 'TJ . . .'

'No need to thank me,' he grinned, as they sat on a pile of old pallets.

'Look, I appreciate the thought,' Selina began, 'but what's the point? I can't exactly fight *you*, can I? It's not about the training, it's about the competition – going up against another fighter. That's when the blood pumps fastest. Am I going to train to be the greatest fighter the world has never seen?'

TJ's heart sank. She was right. 'I'd never thought of that,' he admitted. Neither had Jana. They'd both just imagined that having a new, secret dojo could make up for not being able to fight in public.

Selina smiled, just a little. 'But you thought of me and I'm grateful.'

TJ smiled back. They were sitting side by side, looking into each other's eyes, and if he leaned in just a little closer . . .

'Er – come on,' Selina said, breaking the moment as she stood up. 'We'd better get back before my mum books the wedding reception.'

They left the den and headed back home as the sun began to set over the city. They walked down the steps of an old church and through a tunnel where TJ often came to practise on his board. He imagined what it would be like if he had to give that up and felt another pang of sympathy for the girl beside him. TJ could tell Selina was still unhappy, but it felt as if they were closer, somehow. Better friends than they had been before, maybe.

'I thought I could help,' he told her sadly.

'I'm not sure anyone could help,' Selina admitted. She stopped for a moment, turning to him. 'My dad used to fight too. He was good. Actually he was great. We'd spar every day but he made me give it up when the wolf appeared. I think something happened years ago. Someone tried to hurt my mum and he lost it. Veined up in public. They had to leave everything they had and run. They moved here and then I was born.'

'Like father, like daughter . . .'

'Yeah,' she agreed. 'He encouraged me to learn, but always made me promise to give it up after my first transformation.' Selina twined her fingers together, biting her lip guiltily. 'If they knew I was still practising they would freak.'

They started walking again, both falling silent as they wove through the passageways created by the sandstone walls. The sunlight was slowly fading, casting long, low shadows against the pale yellow paths.

'Sorry I killed the vibe,' Selina sighed, as the silence stretched. 'Hey,' she said suddenly. 'You know what

116

would be great? We should go to the woods one night and wolf out. Get our kicks the way a Wolfblood should!'

TJ screwed up his face. 'I can't . . .'

'Oh, come on,' she said, rolling her eyes. 'I thought you were the rebellious type?'

'No,' TJ said, stopping her with a hand on her arm and making her look at him. 'I don't think you under-stand. I *can't* . . .'

'Can't?' Selina looked at him, finally realising what he was saying. 'Oh! But –'

'Yeah, yeah, I know,' he said, embarrassed. 'Now you're going to say, "It'll happen, TJ", and "When the time is right, TJ", and "There's so much more about being a Wolfblood than wolfing out, TJ" . . . It's cool. I know everyone is different and some things take longer . . .'

TJ stopped speaking when he realised Selina wasn't paying any attention whatsoever. She was looking over his shoulder at something behind him instead.

'Oi,' he protested. 'I'm pouring my heart out here and you're not even listening!'

Selina pushed past him. 'Hey!' she yelled. 'Get off her!'

TJ turned to see a man grabbing at an old lady's bags. At Selina's yell he took off, still clutching her handbag. Selina ran after him.

'Selina!' TJ yelled. He ran to the old lady to see if she was all right and then chased after his friend.

Selina kept on the thief's tail as he careened down some steep steps beside the graveyard and swung a sharp left. If he thought he could lose Selina that easily, though, he was mistaken. He turned another corner and then another, eventually finding himself in a dead end as three walls covered in old graffiti trapped him in. He swung around, breathing hard, only to find Selina and TJ blocking his escape.

'Drop the bag and you can go,' Selina said in a low voice.

'Get out of my way,' the mugger told her.

'Sel?' TJ asked, worried.

'I've so got this,' she said, sounding utterly confident.

TJ grinned as he realised that she really did have this. He pulled out his phone. 'Oh, this is going to be *good*.'

Selina pulled her scarf up to cover her face as TJ started filming. 'Don't forget,' she told the thug. 'I gave you the chance to walk away . . .'

The mugger didn't stand a chance. TJ watched in awe as Selina ducked and dived, pivoted and struck. The thief thought he had her when she turned her back. He lunged at her, but Selina just ran up the wall and backflipped over his head. The mugger stopped dead, shocked. Then he dropped the bag and made a run for it. He clearly knew when he was beaten.

'That was awesome!' TJ laughed, as the thief's fleeing footsteps echoed into the distance.

'We should return this,' Selina said, holding up the stolen handbag with a grin. Then she saw TJ's phone. 'TJ, put it away! What if someone sees?'

'That was amazing!' TJ enthused. 'I am going to share this on every social network known to man and Wolfblood!'

'Don't you dare,' Selina warned. 'If my parents see it . . .'

'You can't tell it's you,' he pointed out, completely enthused. 'I can see it: you standing on top of a building at the end, sirens, jumping into action on your next mission!'

'Ha!' Selina said, and then added, 'We do need more female superheroes . . .'

'You!' TJ exclaimed, getting into the idea. 'All you need is a costume and a cool name!'

'And a sappy sidekick who I have to keep saving?' she suggested playfully, batting him away.

'I'm serious!' TJ insisted. 'You're like a ninja. You could be a real superhero!'

Selina shook her head, but she was smiling. TJ took that as a win.

Eleven

TJ did put the video up. First, though, he shot more footage of Selina doing her stuff around the city. He filmed her as she flicked some amazing kicks from the wrought-iron railings of the High Bridge. He watched in awe, using his phone to film her backflipping over low walls and vaulting down steps that he wouldn't have even been able to jump on his skateboard.

She was just *awesome*.

Something had happened since the night Selina had stopped the thug from stealing the old lady's handbag. TJ felt that they were closer – better friends. They had a secret that only they shared, and that was cool. OK, so Selina still didn't seem to want to get any closer than just friends, but he could deal with that. TJ just liked hanging out with her. And all the time she was hanging out with him, she was distracted from the fact that she couldn't do tae kwon do, which meant that she also wasn't in danger of veining up in public. It wouldn't matter if she wolfed out a bit. No one was going to see. Which meant no one needed to know. Did they?

So when he posted the video, TJ didn't really think

anything of it. Selina always covered her face with a scarf anyway – and sure, there were a few shots where he'd caught Selina's eyes glowing yellow, but that wasn't a problem. It wasn't as if anyone other than them really knew about the video anyway. It had only been viewed a handful of times, and most of those were TJ re-watching it himself. No one else was taking any notice.

Except that then they did.

A local vlogger called Jack had found the video and shared a post that linked to it from his own much more popular site. He'd also added his own commentary . . . and that was where TJ and Selina's problems began.

'Who is this amazing girl and why do her eyes glow?' said Jack's voice, echoing into the darkness of the den from the little screen on TJ's phone. 'They're like a cat's, or a wolf's . . . Like a *she-wolf*!'

TJ glanced at Selina, wondering what her reaction was going to be. 'I think you just got famous . . .'

Selina was amazed and also a little excited. She watched the video again, then checked to see how many people had linked back to the original video since the blog had gone up. 'Look at the traffic on your site!' she said. 'We had about ten people last week, now thanks to him there's hundreds!'

TJ was pacing, nervous. 'It'll be fine,' he said, aloud. 'Segolia won't notice. Are they going to notice? No, it'll definitely be fine. It's going to be fine.' He stopped pacing and looked at Selina. 'Isn't it?'

'One local vlogger noticed my eyes go yellow and he's not exactly Zoella,' Selina pointed out. 'Besides, half the comments on here think the eyes are contact lenses.'

TJ was mainly worried about something else. 'My mum's definitely going to find out.'

Selina shrugged. 'She's got bigger problems than me, TJ.'

TJ wasn't sure about that. 'I guess but . . . "she-wolf"?'

Selina grinned. 'I know. It's pretty cool, right?'

'If you say so . . .'

'It means I can make a difference,' she told him, happier than he'd seen her in a while.

TJ tried to ignore the sick, worried feeling in his stomach. 'I've got to go,' he said. 'Mum's expecting me back.'

Selina handed back his phone with a smile. 'See you tomorrow, yeah? And don't stress. It'll be fine!'

TJ headed home, wishing he could be as excited about this as Selina. He opened the door and shrugged off his coat, dumping it on the hallway floor.

'Pick it up, TJ!' yelled his mum's voice.

TJ stopped. 'How does she even know?' he muttered, scooping up his jacket and hanging it on a peg.

He found her in the kitchen, looking at her iPad with an anxious look on her face.

'What's up?' he asked.

'Come and look at this video,' said his mum.

TJ felt instantly cold. He had the feeling he knew exactly what she was looking at.

'What video? Unless it's a bulldog on a skateboard, I'm not interested. Have you seen that? Let me show you . . .'

He went to pull the iPad towards him, but his mum held on to it. 'This is serious, TJ. I think this "She-wolf" could be a Wolfblood – and local. Have you heard anything?'

'Not a thing. Haven't even seen it,' TJ lied through his teeth as he glanced at Selina's yellow eyes looking back at him from the screen. He tried not to let his internal panic show. 'Anyway, I reckon that's just contacts or visual effects.'

His mum shook her head. 'No. Something's off.'

TJ shrugged. 'I'll keep my ear to the ground,' he said, before making an excuse so that he could get out of there.

The next day, though, things got even worse. The tae kwon do tournament was due to happen after school and TJ knew Selina would need something to distract her from the thought of Hannah winning the trophy. But when she cornered him and showed him something on his phone, he wasn't convinced that what she'd found was the right way to handle it.

'TJ, check this out,' she said, holding up her phone.

'A little girl, Lauren, left a comment on our site. She needs our help.'

'Look, Sel – my mum has seen the videos.'

'Her dog's been stolen and the kidnappers are demanding a ransom,' Selina said, as if she hadn't even heard him.

TJ made a face. 'Why would someone do that? Sel, my mum is on the case –'

Selina held up the screen, showing a picture of the missing dog. 'Look! How cute? And sad!'

'Are you listening to me?' TJ asked, exasperated.

'I got it,' Selina said impatiently. 'Your mum is going to investigate. But we can help this girl. What if they don't give Lauren her dog back? What if they sell it on, or worse?'

'Then the police can handle it!'

'She's too scared to go to the police,' Selina told him. She folded her arms, decided. 'We're getting the puppy back.'

'How are you going do that?'

'We go with her.'

'It's a dark moon tomorrow!'

'Then we go tonight,' Selina said. 'I'll message her back.'

TJ shook his head. 'I'm not going to be there and I think I'm going to take the site down. Look,' he sighed, at Selina's expression of shock, 'you know it's serious if *I'm* being the sensible one.'

124

'But we're a team!' she protested.

'If we were, you would have asked what I thought or at least pretended to hear what I said,' he pointed out.

'I'm not letting this girl down,' Selina insisted. 'I'll go alone.'

TJ was hurt. He'd thought they were friends, that they were in this together, but . . . 'Your choice,' he shrugged, before walking away.

He tried to talk to Jana again, to finally admit that he'd lied when he'd said Selina's problems were sorted, but the Kafe was too busy. So there was only one thing for it. He'd have to deal with this himself. Somehow . . .

Selina had arranged to go with Lauren to confront her puppy's kidnapper. The meet had been set up for that evening, at an old abandoned warehouse in the industrial part of the city. Selina got there early, creeping inside the large, empty building without a sound. Once inside she realised she should have brought a torch – the place was very dark. It had once been a meat-packing factory and its rooms and passageways were cold and dank. Plastic sheeting still hung here and there where it had once divided up the factory lines. It flapped spookily as she made her way deeper inside.

Selina sniffed, but there was no sign of the little girl.

'Lauren?' she called, quietly, finally catching a scent. With her sharp wolf vision she saw a figure silhouetted through a sheet of plastic. She crept towards it, though Selina already knew that it definitely wasn't a little girl. It was someone else, waiting for her here in the shadows . . .

Selina slipped up behind the hooded figure and dropped a hand on to its shoulder. 'Boo!' she hissed into its ear.

TJ spun around, clearly scared. He scowled when he saw who it was. 'What did you do that for?'

Selina shrugged. 'I thought you'd given up on me.'

'I never said that. I just think you need to be much more careful.'

'So you've got your camera?'

TJ looked awkward. 'No. I'm not taking that risk any more.'

Selina sighed. 'Why are you even here?'

'Why do you think?' TJ asked her. There was a brief, uncomfortable silence. Then he said, 'We're a team.'

Selina nodded down the empty corridor. 'I've picked up a scent. Someone was here before you. Come on, this way . . .'

They hadn't gone very far before they saw a figure ahead of them – too tall to be Lauren, it had to be the dognapper.

'It's him!' Selina hissed, dragging her scarf up to hide her face as they crept forward.

They rounded a corner, but the figure had vanished.

'Where did he go?' TJ asked.

Selina shook her head – she'd lost the scent. There

was no sign of the figure, but in the middle of the room was Lauren's puppy. It was tiny and scared, yelping and barking as TJ went to it.

'Aw, it's all right,' TJ told it, picking the dog up. 'Come on, let's get you home, eh?'

'Something's not right,' Selina said, unmasking with a frown as she looked around. 'Come on, let's go.'

TJ followed her, but they'd only gone a few steps when a flash blinded them. It was a camera! Selina blinked as the photographer snapped a series of photographs and then ran.

'Oi!' she yelled, giving chase.

'Oh no . . .' said TJ, realising that Selina didn't have her face covered.

Selina caught up with the figure, tripping him so that he and the camera went flying. She was veining up, her eyes yellow and her teeth bared as she towered over the person cowering on the ground.

TJ recognised him straight away. It was Jack, the vlogger who had called Selina a she-wolf. He was older than both TJ and Selina, but right then he was shaking like a leaf, utterly terrified as Selina crouched over him, snarling, her wolf rising to the surface without her even realising it.

'Argh! Please, please don't hurt me!,' he begged, holding up his hands to shield himself. 'I-I swear I won't say anything to anyone!'

'What happened to Lauren?' Selina yelled.

'There was no Lauren! It's my dog! I wanted to know who you were. Please don't hurt us. Here!' He thrust the camera at Selina, trying to get her to take it, but she carried on growling.

'Sel, enough,' TJ said, putting down the puppy and dragging her away from Jack. 'Get off him!'

The puppy ran to its owner. TJ took the camera, removing the memory card before throwing the camera back to Jack. The vlogger scrabbled to catch it, holding the dog close, still terrified.

Selina backed away, letting the wolf fade as she realised how close she'd come to attacking the vlogger. 'I never meant . . .'

'Look, I didn't even see anything,' Jack said, still terrified. 'Please don't hurt us . . . And – and I'll never mention the she-wolf again.'

'You swear?' TJ asked.

'I swear,' Jack promised.

TJ nodded. Then he pulled Selina out of the room, leaving the vlogger alone.

They left the abandoned building in silence. Outside, there was just a thin sliver of moon hanging in the night sky, barely there at all.

'Did you see what I did to him?' Selina muttered, clearly shocked at herself.

'I tried to tell you . . .' TJ said.

'I thought I was doing good,' she said.

128

'You were,' TJ told her. 'But now you have to stop.'

'He saw my wolf,' she whispered, sounding scared. That worried TJ more than anything else. He'd never seen Selina scared of anything.

'He doesn't know who you are.' TJ touched her arm briefly, trying to reassure her. Selina looked up at him with sad, worried eyes. Then she walked away, into the darkness. TJ watched her go, feeling awful. He'd thought he could deal with this himself. He'd thought he could help Selina. But he hadn't. He'd just made everything worse.

And she was *still* veining up.

Twelve

A dark moon is a Wolfblood's worst nightmare. The lack of moon takes away every drop of wolf in them. It weakens them, sapping their energy. Jana, for example, went from zipping around the Kafe like a livewire to lying in bed, unable to move. Katrina was unimpressed, but Jana just pulled the duvet over her head and went back to sleep.

Selina wasn't faring any better, especially since as soon as she got to school, Hannah and her cronies were right up in her face, waving the trophy that Hannah had won in the tournament.

'You should have come last night,' Hannah taunted. 'You could have learned something.'

Selina said nothing. She didn't trust herself enough.

'Are you OK?' TJ asked her, as Hannah went on her way with a cocky grin on her face.

'I've been better,' Selina muttered. 'The dark moon isn't really helping.'

'Good news is, Jack stuck to his word,' TJ said. 'His whole vlog channel has been deactivated.'

That didn't make Selina feel any better. 'Great,' she

sighed. 'I freaked him out so much he's given up the thing he obviously loved. I wanted to help people, not harm them.'

TJ shrugged. 'It's done,' he said. 'We're in the clear.'

TJ couldn't blame Selina for being upset. But he also couldn't think of another way to help her, either. Not like Jana – she always knew what to do. And now, TJ knew what he had to do. What he should have done in the first place – tell Jana the truth. The first chance he got, he went over to the Kafe. Katrina was on her own, bustling around with an air of annoyance as she tried to deal with customers by herself.

He found Jana lying on the sofa, half-buried under a duvet, looking pale and drawn. 'You look terrible,' he told her, perching beside her.

'Thanks,' Jana said wryly. 'I feel worse . . .' She sighed. 'I've been neglecting you and the pack in favour of lattes and two-for-one specials on cupcakes! Is everything all right?'

TJ felt so relieved that he could finally talk to her that he didn't know how to begin. To her credit, Jana didn't have a go at him for lying to her. She just listened, and then thought for a bit.

'I once punished Aran for something, even though he didn't deserve it,' she said eventually. 'He and Meinir were threatening my position as alpha. I lied, and I couldn't live with the guilt. I couldn't sleep. I was veining up all night. Maybe lying to her parents is affecting Selina in the same way.'

TJ frowned. 'So . . . Selina's veining up because she feels bad?'

'Guilty,' Jana corrected. 'Angry at herself. You've seen with Carrie what it can do to someone. Selina's guilt has been building up and it needs somewhere else to go –'

'And she wolfs out!' TJ exclaimed. 'Jana – you are a genius!' He leaned over and gave her a sloppy kiss on the cheek before bounding up out of the chair.

'Er – well, we really need to talk about what's appropriate behaviour around your alpha,' said Jana, making a face as she wiped the spot where his kiss had landed.

'Oh, whatever,' said TJ, heading for the door.

Jana sighed, shook her head, and snuggled back under the duvet.

Selina had gone straight home from school and got into bed, which was where her mum found her that evening.

'Dark moons don't last forever,' Sophia said. 'You'll feel better in the morning.'

'No, I won't,' Selina told her mum. 'Because I'm a liar, a cheat and a fraud and I deserve to feel like this.'

'Has something happened between you and TJ?' Mrs Khan asked, as Selina's dad appeared in the doorway.

'Hey,' said her dad. 'What's this?'

Selina sat up, slowly, knowing that the time for the

truth had finally come. She couldn't bottle it up any more.

Her parents sat on the bed beside her. Her mum squeezed Selina's leg, just as if Selina was still a little cub. It almost made Selina want to cry.

'Mum, I'm sorry. I've been lying to you both,' she began. 'I'm not who you think I am . . .'

Then she told them everything. In fact, she'd only just finished when TJ rang the doorbell. Mr Khan went to open the door.

'Aha,' said Selina's dad, as he saw TJ on the doorstep. 'Just the man. I think we need to have a little chat.'

Selina and Mrs Khan appeared behind Mr Khan.

'Selina's told us everything,' said Mrs Khan.

TJ looked at Selina. 'Everything?'

'Everything,' she said.

'*Everything*, everything?' he asked, realising that if that was the case, he was probably in exactly the sort of trouble he'd been trying to avoid.

'Everything,' said Mr Khan pointedly.

TJ gulped.

Next morning, Selina went downstairs to find her mum in the kitchen, cooking a massive, meaty breakfast. She sat down at the table and a huge plate of food appeared in front of her.

'Eat,' said her mum.

Selina picked up her knife and fork. 'I thought you'd be mad at me,' she said, quietly.

Her mum smiled. 'You know what a parent's job really is?'

Selina raised her eyebrows. 'To bang on about doing homework, make you pick up clothes and embarrass you at parties?'

'All that, yes,' her mum agreed. 'But most important, a parent's job is to make sure their child is truly happy. That's all me and your dad really want.'

Selina smiled and they hugged. 'Where is Dad, anyway?' she asked a moment later, tucking into her breakfast.

Her mum grinned. 'He's been busy. There's something you have to see. But eat first!'

Once she'd stuffed herself almost to bursting, her mum led her down into the cellar. Selina looked around, astonished at what she saw. It was a whole dojo, right there in their house – he must have been up all night, building it!

'Dad! What are you doing?'

Her dad smiled at her, spreading his arms. 'Who says the cellar just has to be for full moons?'

Selina shook her head, overwhelmed as she gave him a huge hug. 'Dad . . . this is amazing.'

'This is your life,' her dad told her, hugging back, 'and we want you to fight for what you think is right.'

'Just not crime fighting,' her mum added.

Selina felt tears in her eyes. 'I don't deserve this. I could have hurt that boy.'

'But you didn't,' her dad reminded her.

'Because of TJ,' Selina pointed out.

'No. Because of you, Selina.' He tapped her chest, right over her heart. 'Because of what's in here. You might doubt yourself, but we never will, Selina-san. Now . . . fight!'

'Don't hit too hard,' said her mum.

'I won't,' Mr Khan assured her.

'I wasn't talking to you,' Mrs Khan told him, laughing.

It was the best sparring session Selina had had in weeks.

'Have you guys seen Sel?' TJ asked at school the next morning, as he met Matei and Emilia in the corridor outside their lockers.

'Nope,' said Matei. 'Sorry, mate.'

'You haven't split up, have you?' Emilia asked anxiously.

'What?' TJ said. 'We are not going out!'

Matei and Emilia looked at each other. 'We believe you!' they said together.

At that moment Selina appeared, beaming a huge smile. She ran straight up to TJ and leapt into his arms, hugging him so hard she almost knocked him over.

'Oh!' said TJ, very surprised, as he put her down again. 'Are you OK?'

'I had a proper sparring session this morning – and I didn't start veining!' Selina said, with complete delight.

'My parents said I can even carry on with tae kwon do! I should never have lied to them, TJ. That's what was causing all the problems – the lying.'

Hannah appeared at the end of the corridor, barging straight through the group with her equally nasty gang in tow. 'Sorry,' she said, appearing anything but. 'Didn't know there were losers in my way . . .'

Matei looked as if he might start something, but Emilia held him back. 'She's not worth it,' she told him.

'What did you say about me?' Hannah challenged her.

Emilia wasn't scared. She stared Hannah right in the face. 'I said you're a bully and a cheat and you're not worth it.'

Hannah just laughed. 'Yeah? And what are you going to do about it, hun?'

Selina stepped in front of Emilia, squaring up to Hannah. 'She's not doing anything.'

Hannah smirked. 'Thought so.'

'But I am,' Selina said firmly. 'After school? Me and you, on the mat.'

Hannah sneered. 'You had your chance to win the trophy, Selina. You ran away.'

Selina stood her ground, cool and calm. 'I don't need a trophy. See you in the gym.'

The news about Selina and Hannah's bout went around the school like wildfire. Everyone was talking about it, and when lessons had ended, so many students poured into the gym that every seat was taken. TJ had called Jana and they sat with Matei and Emilia, looking down as Selina prepared for the fight.

'Think she can do this without wolfing out?' Matei asked.

TJ shrugged. 'She says she can . . .'

The referee blew the whistle and the match began. Silence rippled around the gym. Hannah stood on the mat, bouncing on her feet, obviously full of nervous energy. Selina, though, was completely calm, walking slowly towards her opponent.

TJ couldn't help himself. 'Come on, Selina!' he shouted. She turned and winked at him, and that was when TJ knew for sure that everything was going to be just fine.

'Oh, she's so got this,' he muttered, with a grin.

Selina went into the fight with the grace of a dancer and the speed of a hummingbird, yet she hardly even had to make a strike. Hannah threw a hundred punches and kicks, but Selina dodged and somersaulted over every single one, spinning away and dancing back in as she simply let Hannah exhaust herself.

'Break!' called the referee, eventually.

Selina turned her back to re-tie her belt, and Hannah attacked, trying to cheat just as she had before. The referee had no time to stop her, but it didn't matter. Selina felt her opponent coming and flipped herself over

137

Hannah's head, letting the other girl's momentum send her sprawling to the floor. Selina loomed over Hannah, who was red-faced and breathing hard.

'Enough!' Hannah gasped. 'I can't carry on.'

Selina looked at her for a second, and then offered Hannah a hand to help her up. The two girls faced each other and bowed respectfully.

'You won,' Hannah admitted, reaching for the tae kwon do trophy, intending to hand it to her opponent.

Selina wouldn't take it. 'You won that fair and square,' she said. She turned around to look up at her friends in the stands. TJ, Jana, Matei and Emilia were all cheering and laughing. Selina smiled. 'I've got what I need.'

Thirteen

A few days later, Selina called a meeting. There was something important she thought they should all talk about and she wanted everyone to be there, including Jana. They arranged to meet at the den once school was over – Selina, TJ, Matei and Emilia got there ahead of Jana, who had told them she needed to finish her shift at the Kafe first.

'So what's this about?' Matei asked, as he settled himself on a pile of old pallets.

'Well, I don't want to make things awkward for the pack,' said Selina. 'But that is what we are now, isn't it? A pack. So . . . it's time we made someone alpha. Properly.'

TJ's heart sank as he realised what she meant. 'Now?'

'You don't have to stay if you feel weird,' Selina told him gently.

'Why would I feel weird?' TJ asked, too quickly. Selina just looked at him. He knew she wasn't going to say it, but of course there was a reason that he'd feel weird – a very good reason. TJ knew exactly what was going to happen next, and he couldn't be a part of it. He wanted the ground to swallow him up, there and then.

139

Jana walked in. 'Hey,' she said, seeing everyone gathered together. 'What's the emergency?'

Selina, Matei and Emilia all dropped on to one knee in front of Jana, placing one hand on the ground and holding the other in the air towards her in the time-honoured sign of Wolfblood submission. TJ slowly followed suit.

'Oh . . .' Jana said, with a smile, realising what was happening. 'OK . . .' She dropped to the floor, accepting their obeisance.

One by one, the pack transformed. Jana's eyes yellowed and her veins flooded black, her teeth growing into fangs as she growled. The others followed suit, still facing Jana as their wolf-selves came to the surface.

TJ's eyes yellowed and he growled, baring his teeth just as they had, but his body remained frustratingly human. The Wolfblood in his veins sparked just as it always did, but did not ignite properly. He was still just TJ. Boring, non-wolf TJ. *Still.* It was humiliating. More than that, it wasn't *fair*.

TJ got up, hanging his head and feeling wretched. How could he be part of accepting their new alpha when he wasn't even a proper Wolfblood? He stood at the back of the newly formed pack, staring at the ground.

Wolf-Jana padded across the concrete floor of the den and stood before him, looking up with her wise yellow wolf eyes. He knew she was trying to be kind, trying to

140

make sure he was included, but right then it didn't make TJ feel any better at all.

Not even one of Katrina's outstanding cheeseburgers helped lift TJ's funk.

'No girlfriend today?' Katrina asked brightly, as he walked into the Kafe. 'You know, the one who does the feng shui fighting?'

TJ sighed. 'She's not –'

'She is *totally* into you,' Katrina said, cutting him off. 'I've got a fifth sense for these things. You should ask her out.'

She headed off, leaving TJ even more depressed. *Yeah, sure,* he thought. *The ultra-cool kung fu Wolfblood girl is really going to go for the unable-to-wolf-out boy.*

Then he saw something so beautiful that he completely forgot to feel sorry for himself. It was a pair of the most amazing trainers he'd ever seen in his life, worn by a girl who was standing at the jukebox. She was dressed head to toe in sportswear and staring intently at her phone. TJ stared, gobsmacked.

'Please tell me those are *not* original vintage,' he said, leaning closer. She ignored him but TJ wasn't put off. Those trainers were just too special. 'Eighties all-white high-tops! They are so rare they hardly exist! How'd you even *know* about those?'

This time the girl sighed and rolled her eyes, which he

141

chose to take as a good sign. TJ leaned beside her against the jukebox with a grin. 'You've got to be another trainer nut,' he said. 'I *never* meet trainer nuts. I can*not* talk to my friends about this stuff. They'd rather eat a trainer than wear one. Some of them have.'

The girl looked up. She was pretty, with pale skin, olive green eyes and long dark hair flowing out from beneath the grey wool beanie she'd pulled down over her ears. It was his lucky day.

'OK,' he said, figuring that this was a definite case of nothing ventured, nothing gained, 'I'm sounding crazy here, but I'm not. My name is TJ. That actually stands for "True Gentleman". My mum can't spell.' She actually smiled at that. A smile! 'So you've got to tell me where you found them. And if they had another pair two sizes up? And . . . what you're doing for the rest of your life?'

It was that moment that the others turned up, led by Jana. She, Selina, Matei and Emilia were just in time to see the girl reach up with an eyeliner pencil and write something right in the middle of TJ's forehead. It was her name and a number.

'Anything to stop you talking,' she said, with another slight smile. Then she left.

'What's it say?' TJ asked once she'd gone, pointing to his forehead as the others all slid into a booth. 'Is it rude? Is it going to come off?' He got out his phone and held up the selfie camera to his face so he could see it.

'You got her number,' Selina told him, obviously a bit surprised.

'Her name's Niamh! And I got her number!' said TJ, astonished. The others stared at him. 'What?'

Matei raised his eyebrows. 'She's human.'

TJ shrugged. 'So?'

'You want to get with another Wolfblood,' Jana told him. She felt Matei watching her and couldn't help looking at him. He smiled at her and Jana felt herself beginning to blush. This had been happening a lot lately. They'd glance at each other just a second too long . . . She turned away quickly, ignoring the tiny extra thump of her heart.

'I don't think your mum would like it much,' Emilia added, completely oblivious to the silent conversation going on between her brother and her brand-new alpha.

'My mum is not the boss of me,' TJ declared, just as his phone started to ring. He answered it and held it to his ear. It was his mum. 'Yeah, I'll let her know. Straight away, yeah. *Yes*, I'll get the steaks. By five, *yeah*!'

He hung up to find the rest of them sniggering at him. 'Mum says to tell you to come to ours,' he said to Jana.

Jana tried to talk him out of calling Niamh as they made their way home.

'You're not really going to go through with this?' she asked, as TJ stared at Niamh's number in his phone, trying to pluck up the courage to call or text.

'Look,' said TJ, 'you might be happy being sad and single, but I'm not.'

'Oi!' Jana protested. 'Who says I haven't had boyfriends?'

'Matei doesn't count.'

Jana felt the blush she'd been trying to hide earlier come flooding back. 'I don't know what you mean.'

'Yeah, yeah. Course not,' said TJ, as if he didn't believe a word she said.

'I'm your alpha now,' she teased him, as they leaned over the railing to look at the river rushing past beneath them. 'You have to at least pretend to believe me, even if you don't!' She thought it best to change the subject. 'OK, so it's not easy finding another Wolfblood, especially in the city. I *get* that –'

'Yeah? Well, try it when you're not really one yourself,' TJ told her, with a touch of bitterness. 'You think Wolfblood girls are into boys who haven't transformed yet?'

'You *will* transform,' Jana told him. 'Then things will get easier. Until then – is it worth the hassle?'

'You're supposed to be all for living side by side, aren't you?'

Jana nodded. 'But not everyone feels the same. Some will be dead against it.'

'What are they going to do?' TJ challenged. 'Eat her?'

Jana sighed. 'Well, if you're going to call, call. Be bold. Alpha-like. Girls love that.'

So he did.

It was difficult to be hard on TJ when he was so hyped up. Jana couldn't help but smile at how bouncy he was after he'd made his phone call. *Good for him*, she thought. *At least someone's love life is working out . . .* She tried not to think about why Matei's face seemed to pop into her head at that moment.

When they got to TJ's house, Imara was sitting at the table with a book. She didn't say hello or smile. Instead she held up the book. Jana could see from the cover that it was called *Bloodwolf*. Then Imara started to read aloud.

'"When a wild red-haired girl comes to the village of Rockybridge, no one knows that on a full moon she transforms into a wild beast –"' she began

'What?' Jana said, startled. Imara carried on.

'"Or of her secret love for the handsome young Bloodwolf Gideon –"'

'*What?*' Jana said again, grabbing the book. She turned it over. There was a picture of the author on the back. The man was trying to look sophisticated. He wasn't doing a very good job.

Jana knew exactly who it was. The last time she'd seen him he'd been standing in front of a whiteboard in her final ever class at Bradlington High. The picture was of Mr Jeffries, her old history teacher.

TJ took Niamh to the skate park for the start of their first date. He wanted to impress her. Any girl who was that into trainers was sure to be bowled over by a few goofy-foots and the odd Caballerial. And also, he *might* have looked at her Instagram . . . It had been full of pictures of her on a skateboard.

'Told you I was good,' he said, coasting to a stop in front of her.

Niamh shook her head. 'Good?' she said. 'Unreal! How'd you do that?'

TJ wondered if he'd gone a bit too far. 'Er . . . YouTube videos . . .' She smiled at him, but still looked at bit suspicious. He hurried things along. 'I haven't seen what you can do yet.'

'Told you, I'm injured. How'd you even know I was into boarding?'

He grinned. 'Awesome judge of female character.'

'Or you snooped me.'

TJ shrugged. 'You really should have everything set to private . . .'

'I snooped you too. Tried, anyway. Couldn't find one thing.'

'What can I say? Man of mystery . . .' He tried to lean in for a kiss, but she stopped him.

'It's a bit weird though,' she pointed out. 'Almost like you've got something to hide.'

'Only my ridiculous good looks,' he said, but her face said she wasn't having it. TJ sighed. 'My mum won't let me do social media.'

Niamh laughed a bit at that, but only for a second. 'Seriously, I don't like secrets,' she said. 'I need you to be upfront with me.'

'Sure,' he said. He tried to kiss her again, but she ducked and jogged away, laughing.

They went to the Kafe. TJ wanted to introduce her to his friends properly, and he was pretty sure it was where they'd be. They were, too – all except Jana, anyway.

'Hey! I wanted you guys to meet properly,' TJ said, as he and Niamh walked up to their usual booth. 'Matei, Selina, Emilia . . . This is Niamh.'

'Hey,' Niamh said, as TJ went to get them some drinks from the counter. 'So how do you know TJ?'

'We're at the same school,' Emilia told her.

Niamh smiled. 'Oh – so you know all his terrible secrets?'

Matei stood up. 'Emilia, we need to get home.'

Emilia stood, a bit awkwardly. A second later Selina did the same. 'Er – me too. It was nice to meet you . . .'

'Hey, where are you all going?' TJ asked as they left.

'I don't think they liked me,' said Niamh.

'I have weird friends,' TJ admitted. 'I should have told you *how* weird.'

Niamh nodded. 'Did you order yet?'

'Er, no.'

'Sit,' she said. 'My treat.'

She left her phone on the table and went up to the counter. It pinged as TJ sat down – a text, flashing up on screen. TJ glanced at it, and then frowned. He reached out and picked it up, reading what the message said with a horrible, burning feeling in his chest.

STAY AWAY FROM HIM. OR YOU WILL GET HURT.

He stared at it, almost not believing it for a second. It had to mean him, didn't it? The 'him' Niamh was supposed to stay away from was TJ. But why? And who would send something like that? The number had been withheld. He glanced over his shoulder to where Niamh was at the counter, being served by Katrina. His thumb hovered over the delete button. He shouldn't have been looking at her phone as it was. Deleting a message before she'd seen it – that was *really* bad. But . . . he didn't want her to see that. Why should she? Whoever had sent the message was the one in the wrong. But who could have sent it? Who *would* have? It wouldn't have been one of his friends, would it? Not one of *his* pack? But who else –

TJ didn't even want to think about that.

He pressed delete just as Niamh turned to come back to the table.

She frowned slightly as she saw her phone in his hand. 'Were you looking at my phone?'

'Oh, I – I was just thinking about getting one of these,' he explained quickly.

TJ tried to push his anger and worry away, but it hung over him like a cloud for the rest of their date. That made him even more annoyed, because if it hadn't been for the text, everything would have been brilliant. Niamh was easy to talk to once you got past her chilly exterior. Besides, they had loads in common.

Later, once they'd left the Kafe, TJ wondered what he was supposed to do next. It wasn't as if he'd had much experience with dates. Should he try to take her hand, or kiss her properly, or what? The last time he'd properly tried to kiss a girl had been Selina, and that hadn't exactly been a success, had it?

'So . . . I don't know which way you're going, but I could walk you home,' he said.

Niamh rolled her eyes. 'Do I look like I need walking home?'

TJ grinned. 'I'm not worried about you getting attacked – it's what you'll do to *them* that bothers me.'

She laughed and elbowed him in the ribs. TJ grinned back. Suddenly they were standing very close together. He leaned in –

Her phone buzzed and Niamh pulled it out. She frowned at the screen. 'What's *that* meant to mean?' She held it up for him to see.

RUN NOW WHILE YOU STILL CAN.

TJ swallowed. 'Probably a wrong number,' he managed.

'There's no reason for me to run from you, is there?' she asked. 'There's nothing I need to know?'

Right then, TJ wanted to tell her the truth. Just for a second, he thought about it, but . . . He shrugged. 'What you see is what you get.'

Niamh looked at him for another minute. 'Well . . . You don't seem like much of a threat . . .'

She leaned in and kissed him. After a surprised second, TJ kissed her back. Then Niamh stepped away with a grin.

'Call me,' she said, and ran off.

Fourteen

Jana had managed to persuade Imara to let her deal with Mr Jeffries. Whatever he was playing at, he'd proved in the past he could be trusted. But she couldn't believe how stupid he'd been, and she made sure he knew that straight away.

'What were you thinking?' Jana asked impatiently, as she stood in his kitchen back in Stoneybridge while he made tea. She shook the book at him. 'This is *my* story! Kaddy! Sharron! Tam! You haven't even changed my name, you've just spelled it with a Y! Oh, you disguised Segolia brilliantly though. *Selogia!* No one's ever going solve *that* puzzle, are they? How could you do this to me?'

Mr Jeffries stood quietly for a moment, looking at her. Then he grinned. 'It's so good to see you again, Jana.'

Jana sighed. 'You too, sir.'

'Look,' he said. 'I discovered I'd been teaching a pack of shape-changing creatures. I was chased by black ops people. I genuinely thought I was going to be dog food on several occasions . . . And it was the best thing that had ever happened to me!'

Jana shook her head. 'You need to get out more, sir.'

'Then you all left,' Jeffries went on. 'Everything went back to normal – and normal isn't good enough now. I was part of something; I made a difference. I could stand in front of a class every day for another twenty years and never feel that again.'

Jana shook her head. 'You don't have a life, so you had to steal mine?'

'Have you even read *Bloodwolf*?'

'My boss read it,' she told him. 'That's what matters. I'm here to tell you to take it off sale. Or someone bigger and scarier will come and tell you.'

Jeffries blinked, but still looked determined. 'I'm going to be giving a reading at the church hall by the station at eleven a.m. tomorrow,' he told her.

Jana crossed her arms. It was clear he wasn't going to change his mind. She thought back to how Jeffries had been when he'd first found out about Wolfbloods – scared and unwilling to believe the truth. How things had changed.

Jana went to the reading. She sat at the back of a hall full of ladies with grey hair and listened as Mr Jeffries read out her story. Hearing it written by someone else was very strange. The audience listened politely, but they didn't seem outraged, or terrified.

'This is from the end of the book,' said Mr Jeffries as he concluded the session. He took a breath and looked over at her before he began to read. '"The teacher watched as Yana walked away, into the Selogia building. In her, he saw a leader – a natural alpha. He thought again about her vision of a future where humans and blood-wolves are not enemies. And he knew that she would never allow some faceless corporation to compromise that. She would never let others use her for their own ends. She would always be true to her wolf."'

As Mr Jeffries shut his book, Jana recognised that he'd been thinking about the Jana of the past when he wrote that paragraph. She wondered whether she was still the same. She hoped she was, but feared the city – that Segolia – had changed her.

'Oh – you might have noticed that I have a young friend with me today,' Mr Jeffries added, as the audience's applause died away. 'I just want to introduce her, her name is Jana – she's a Wolfblood. The one I based the book on.'

The room fell silent. Jana stared in utter horror at Mr Jeffries while the rest of the room looked at her.

Then, quietly, politely, the audience began to laugh. A joke! They'd thought he'd been making a joke! Jana watched them all file out of the hall, talking quietly among themselves. None of them even gave her a second chance.

'What was that?' Jana hissed, once they'd all gone and she and Jefferies were alone in the dusty, echoing room.

'This book is not an attack on Wolfbloods,' he told her.

153

'It's a defence. Tell people it's make-believe and they won't believe the truth even when it's staring them in the face.' Jeffries sighed. 'Look, this is your call. If you stick to the party line, I'll have to kill the book. I can't fight Segolia. But if I were you I'd be asking why your boss really sent you. You think she felt threatened by my seventeen sales? Or the fact that you still have human friends?'

Jana thought about that for a moment, and then smiled. 'Fancy coming back with me? Catch up with Katrina?'

Mr Jeffries smiled back. 'How could I resist?'

Niamh continued to get threatening texts. In fact, they got worse and worse. She showed them to TJ the next day when they met up at the skate park after school.

'"I told you stay away from him,"' she read out, '"I said you'd get hurt and you didn't listen. He will have you for lunch."' Niamh shook her head as she looked up at him. 'What does *that* mean, TJ?'

The last one made TJ stop dead, anger washing over him like a tide. Just that morning Matei had made a joke about eating humans.

'Better take some ketchup,' Matei had said, when TJ had told him he was going to meet Niamh again. 'I hear humans are pretty tasteless.'

Fury began to boil in TJ's veins. 'Wait here,' he told Niamh. He was going to sort this out, once and for all.

He ran across town at wolf speed, all the way to the

154

den where he knew the others would be. TJ marched in, angrier than he'd ever been in his life. Selina was there giving Emilia a sparring lesson, but TJ ignored them both completely. He barged between the two girls, lunging towards where Matei was sitting and punching him straight in the face. Matei didn't even have time to put his hands up – the blow knocked him straight to the floor.

'It stops right now,' TJ barked, as Matei scrambled to his feet and Selina grabbed TJ's arms, trying to drag him back. 'I know it's you. Admit it!'

'Get a hold of your wolf,' Selina shouted, as TJ struggled away from her.

TJ snarled again, his eyes fixed on Matei, who was growling back, just as angry.

'It stops NOW,' TJ told him. 'You understand me?'

Then he stalked out of the den.

That wasn't the end of it, though. TJ headed for the Kafe later, trying to find Niamh, but the first person he saw was Matei, sitting alone in the pack's usual booth. His right eye was black and swollen, but TJ didn't even feel sorry for what he'd done. He was still too angry about all the texts that Matei had sent. But then TJ realised that he could smell Niamh's scent lingering in the air. She'd been there – and not long ago, either.

In a flash, TJ knew what the other Wolfblood must have done. Matei obviously *really* didn't want TJ and

Niamh to be together. Scaring Niamh by text hadn't worked so now Matei must be trying a different tactic. TJ couldn't believe it. What was Matei's problem? Was he *jealous*? He couldn't get up the guts to tell Jana he fancied her, so he wanted to ruin things for TJ, too?

'Has she been here?' TJ asked, hackles rising as he went to Matei's table. 'What did you say? You think you've got rid of her, don't you?' he snarled, leaning over Matei where he sat. 'Well, you're wrong. I'm into this girl, right? I mean *massively* into her, and if you wreck it for me by even hinting at you-know-what –'

TJ stopped dead, Niamh's fresh scent wafting to him from the other side of the Kafe. He turned to see her standing at the counter, staring at him. She must have heard everything!

Matei stood up. 'I told her you were a very cool guy,' he said, quiet enough that only TJ could hear. 'You've certainly proved that . . .'

Matei pushed past him and left without another word, leaving TJ to explain things to Niamh.

'There's obviously something you don't want me to find out,' she said. 'Tell me now, or you never see me again.'

TJ tried to find something to say, but even in his head everything he could think of sounded wrong.

'Goodbye,' Niamh told him, turning on her heel.

'Niamh! Wait!' TJ called, but she didn't stop. Then,

suddenly, there was Selina at his elbow. He hadn't even noticed she was in the Kafe.

'It's probably for the best,' she said. 'I didn't like her scent.'

TJ stared after her as Selina walked out of the Kafe, realisation flooding over him. Had it been her, all along? He raced after her, catching up with her by the tables arranged outside.

'You know what? I never had you down as the jealous type,' he said.

Selina looked up at him as if he were mad. '*Sorry?*'

TJ threw up his hands. 'You don't want me, but you don't want anyone else to have me either, is that it? You let me have a go at Matei, too, and all the time –'

'Are you saying *I* sent those messages to your little pet?' Selina spat back at him, just as angry. 'As if I could be *bothered* –'

But TJ had stopped listening. He had just enough time to register that Jana had arrived, accompanied by a human man that TJ didn't recognise. But that wasn't what had caught his attention. TJ stared at the fresh graffiti that had been sprayed over the wall opposite the Kafe.

In huge bold letters it read,

YOU WRECK MY LIFE,
I WRECK YOURS.
CARRIE

TJ ran furiously, leaving Selina and Jana behind. He tried to phone Niamh on his mobile, but there was no answer. As he ended the call TJ spotted one of Niamh's trainers lying beside the road. Then, further on, there was her bag, its contents spilled all over the place. Jana caught up with him as he looked at it, shocked.

'TJ, what's going on?' Jana asked. 'The graffiti said Carrie. Not *morwal* Carrie?'

TJ was trying not to panic. 'I think this is payback,' he said. 'She's been sending texts, saying she'll hurt Niamh – and now I don't know where Niamh is – I can't get her scent . . . What if Carrie's got her?'

'Calm down,' Jana told him. 'Carrie's in Segolia care. I can check on her.'

'Do what you like,' TJ told her, hardly even listening, his face tight with worry. 'I have to find Niamh.'

'TJ!' Jana called after him, but he was already running.

TJ searched all over the place for Niamh. He went to the skate park where he knew she hung out and walked along the river where they had strolled on their first date, but there was no sign of her. He was wracking his brains about what to do when his phone rang in his pocket. The sight of Niamh's name on the screen made his heart almost explode out of his chest with relief.

'Where are you?' he asked.

'She s-said she was watching me,' Niamh stuttered,

sounding terrified. 'She said she knows where I live.'

'Who said?' TJ asked.

'The girl!' Niamh shouted. 'She said she'd rip me apart! What is she talking about? *Why won't you tell me?*'

'I'll explain it,' TJ said, trying to calm her down. 'All of it. Just tell me where you are.'

She told him to go to an old workshop that her dad owned. With Wolfblood speed, TJ was there in minutes. He found a series of rough brick buildings, run down and mostly abandoned or just full of junk. TJ sniffed, searching until he found her scent trail. He followed it through an open door and into a narrow passageway with several doors on either side. Niamh's trail led him to one that was unlocked and slightly open. He peered through the dusty window in the door into a cluttered lock-up stacked with old tins of paint, ladders and dust sheets. There, sitting on the floor with her back to an old work bench, was Niamh. She had her head down, her arms wrapped around her knees.

'Niamh?' he said. 'It's me.' TJ pushed the door open slowly and went to her, putting one arm around her shoulders as he knelt beside her.

'I need to know why this is happening to me right now,' she told him. '*Right now.*'

TJ bit his lip and then took out his phone. Jana should be dealing with this; it was beyond him. 'I think I should call my friend –'

Niamh snatched the phone away. 'No calls. Talk!'

TJ sighed. Didn't he owe Niamh the truth, after everything she'd been through? 'There's this girl,' he began, after a moment. 'Carrie. I think she's after you to – to get back at me. For telling her things that I couldn't deliver on.'

'What things?'

'It's hard to explain,' he said. 'Not without –'

Niamh shook her head in disgust, getting to her feet as TJ followed. 'My *life's* in danger and you still want to keep secrets?'

'I'm a Wolfblood,' TJ blurted out.

'A what?' Niamh asked, confused. She began to back away, edging out of the room.

'I'm not like other people,' TJ tried to explain. 'I . . . I'm faster. Stronger. I change. I'm part-human. Part-wolf. And Carrie – she's like me.'

Niamh stared at him. Then her expression changed. Gone was the panic and confusion of a moment before. She suddenly just looked very, very calm.

'Got you,' she said. Then she slammed shut the door, clamping a padlock on the handle and locking TJ inside. Niamh stared at him through the window.

TJ froze, utterly shocked. 'Niamh! What are you doing? It's not me you have to be scared of, it's Carrie!'

'Carrie didn't send the texts,' Niamh shouted back, 'I sent them to myself! Loads of apps send texts later – it was just planning. Like setting up the fake profiles for you to snoop. Like the graffiti – like *all of it*.'

TJ didn't understand. 'I – I don't –' he stammered.

'Carrie was my best friend!' Niamh raged at him, through the garage door. 'She was totally fixated on you. She went on and on about you – "He's so cool, he likes the coolest music, he's obsessed with trainers . . . " You got her totally into you and then you pushed her over the edge with your made-up Wolfblood nonsense. You put her in hospital. They sent her away and it was all because of *you*! Made you feel big, that, did it? Special? Well, you're not! You're *sick* – and now everyone's going to know it! Her parents, your parents, schools, police, papers, Snapchat, Twitter, Tumblr – the whole world gets to hear *what you did*!'

'Niamh!' TJ shouted desperately. 'You've got it all wrong!'

'There's a webcam on the shelf,' she said, ignoring him. 'When you've made a full confession I'll let you out.'

TJ turned and saw the camera. He leapt at it, feeling his wolf just beneath the surface as his veins blackened and his eyes yellowed.

'Niamh!' he shouted, desperate to get her to listen. '*Niamh!*'

Fifteen

'Niamh!' TJ roared. '*Niamh!*'

He hammered against the door with his fists, desperate to escape. Through the glass window in the door TJ could see her backing away, her phone to her ear. Then she turned and bolted along the passageway, kicking the door at the end shut behind her as she ran outside. Even then, TJ's Wolfblood hearing let him listen to what she was saying.

'Police?' she said, sounding terrified. 'There's – there's something in my dad's lock-up. An animal . . . I don't know what, just send someone now. Please!'

Fear and anger screamed in TJ's veins. He gathered all of his wolf strength and wrenched the garage door clean off its hinges, kicking flurries of dust into the air as it tumbled into the passageway outside. He ran down the corridor and smashed straight into the flimsy wood of the last door between him and Niamh. It splintered around him like firewood as TJ crashed through it.

Niamh screamed and tried to run, but TJ was too fast for her. In a second he had cut off her escape and stood in front of her, snarling.

'End the call,' he yelled. She hesitated, then cut the line with a shaking hand. 'Seriously, Niamh? Is that even your name? Are you totally, completely nutso? How could you lie to my face? Make out that you like me when . . .'

He realised that she was cowering in absolute terror. TJ took a step back and calmed himself down so that his eyes and veins returned to normal.

'You don't have to be afraid of me,' he said, reaching out to touch her arm.

Niamh shrieked and jerked away. 'Get away from me, you freak!' she hissed, holding up her phone. On the screen he could see a clip of him wolfing out. 'Or everyone I know gets *this*!'

'She wants you to take her to *Carrie*?' Jana said in disbelief.

'She won't believe that Carrie's a Wolfblood,' TJ said, his head in his hands as they sat in the den. 'Wants to see with her own eyes. She thinks I've done something to her.'

Jana was trying to stay calm, but this was bad. Very, *very* bad. 'Do you know her real name? Where she lives? *Anything* about her that isn't a lie?'

TJ shook his head miserably. 'I have to tell my mum. She can fix it. That's what she does. Fixes this stuff.'

'And what do you think she'll do to "fix" that girl?'

asked Jana. 'You know what Segolia does – anything, as long as the secret doesn't get out.'

TJ shrugged. 'Who cares? She lied to me and locked me up. Now she's blackmailing me!'

'I'm not blaming you for what she's done, but if anything happens to her, I don't want it on my conscience – do you? Maybe *we* can fix it,' Jana added. 'If we give her what she wants. We'll find Carrie. Show Niamh she's OK. Show her we're not the enemy; persuade her to keep the secret.'

'We don't even know where Carrie is,' TJ pointed out.

'You go back to that garage, see if there's anything there that might tell us who this girl really is,' Jana told him. 'I'll talk to Imara, find out where Carrie is.'

Going back there wasn't really TJ's idea of fun, but it had to be done. The busted door was still lying half in and half out of the room. TJ had to climb over it to get in. The camera in the corner caught his eye as he did so, and he grimaced, wondering if he was still being filmed. He hoped not. After all, not-Niamh had exactly what she needed to make his life a misery already, didn't she?

Not sure where to start, TJ rifled through various crates and stacks of paper before he hit the jackpot. In one battered cardboard box he found a batch of children's paintings, like the ones he used to do with his mum when he was little. One of them showed two small girls, dressed up like princesses. In very wobbly painted writing, someone had written 'Carrie' over one and 'Holly' over the other. Turning the piece of paper over, TJ saw that there was an address written on the other side.

'Gotcha,' he muttered, although it didn't feel like much of a victory.

His phone rang. It was Jana, calling him to report that his mum wasn't going to give up where Carrie was. Something about patient confidentiality.

'Your mum really doesn't want us to know where Carrie is,' Jana sighed. 'Any luck at your end?'

'Her name's Holly,' TJ told her. 'Got an address, too.'

'Good,' said Jana. 'There's another way for me to find Carrie, but I can't do it without Niamh – Holly – whoever she is.'

'What, so we just walk up to her door?' TJ asked, incredulous. 'If she sees us coming she'll think it's an attack and she'll send the video to her friends.'

'*We* don't walk up to her door,' Jana said. 'Someone else does . . .'

Sometimes, Tim Jeffries wondered where it had all gone wrong. All he'd ever really wanted was a quiet life, and then suddenly all this Wolfblood stuff happened. And now here he was, trying to explain to a teenage girl that the world as she knew it – well, wasn't at all as she knew it.

He'd given the girl called Holly a copy of his book, *Bloodwolf*, but she'd shut the door in his face. So he'd resorted to sticking his head through the living-room window while she stood inside, flicking through the novel with utter confusion.

'I get what you're going through,' he said. 'I was scared and confused like you. But I came out the other side. I realised that knowing about them is a privilege.'

She shut the book and turned it over, staring at his photo on the back.

'They're like us,' he went on. 'There are good ones and bad ones. The ones you've met – they're not the bad ones.'

Holly shook her head. 'I don't care who they are – I just want to see my friend.'

'They can't bring Carrie to you,' Jeffries began, holding up his hands as she waved her phone at him threateningly. 'But – they may be able to take you to her.'

She shook her head. 'How naive do you think I am?'

'I will personally vouch for your safety,' he assured her. 'And you can check my ID with anyone you want. Look on my school website. I am a long-serving staff member, very well known. In fact, many former pupils tell me I am their favourite teacher.'

Holly looked at him warily. 'What would I have to do?'

* * *

TJ and Jana were already at the skate park when Jeffries arrived with Holly. TJ could barely keep his anger at bay.

'The video is uploaded to several secure sites,' Holly said immediately, before anyone else could say anything. 'At midnight the password to those sites automatically gets texted to all my friends, unless I cancel it.'

TJ shook his head in disgust. 'Man, drop the super-villain routine!'

'I'll help you,' Jana told the girl, 'but I don't like the way you're doing this.'

Holly didn't seem bothered. 'Why?' she asked. 'Because I pretended to be someone else? Like you do every day?'

Jana ignored that. 'Did you bring something that belonged to Carrie?'

Holly took an old top out of her bag and handed it to Jana. 'I don't see how it can help.'

'It's called Ansion,' Jana told her, as she began to focus on the top. Her eyes yellowed as the mists of the past led her into Carrie's story. There was loud music – Jana could feel a trace of Carrie's past excitement twisting in her own gut as she followed where Ansion was taking her. 'Carrie's not supposed to be there. You neither. Phoning your mum. Can't stop laughing, the both of you. Getting out of uniform. You're putting this top on . . .'

Holly swallowed nervously. 'Carrie loaned me that to go to a concert. We weren't allowed, so we said we were helping at the school –'

167

'School open night,' Jana finished. 'She's . . . worried. She's being taken out of your school and moved to a new one. Her wolf. It's eating her up. She doesn't want it. She needs help. She tries to tell you, but . . .'

Jana abruptly snapped out of Ansion as Holly snatched the top back, breaking her connection.

'You think some mind-reading trick changes things?' Holly hissed, angrily. 'Are you taking me to Carrie or not?'

'I had to make a connection,' Jana explained. 'So now I can do Eolas.' She dropped to the ground, pressing one hand against it, searching for a trace of Carrie in the flow of all things. The vision took her out of the city in a rush of golden light, carrying her into the countryside to a big house surrounded by large, walled grounds. She dived down, looking for the gate. There was a name beside it. Jana tried to read it, but it wasn't easy to make out.

'Carver Hall,' she said, not completely sure.

TJ got his phone out to Google it, but Mr Jeffries' teacher brain was way ahead of them.

'It's *Carter* Hall,' he said.

Sixteen

They needed someone on the inside of Segolia, so they called Doctor Whitewood. She was not best pleased. She arrived at the skate park and slammed the door of her car so hard it sounded like a gunshot.

'I love it when I get a phone call that compromises me in every way,' she said as she marched up to Jana, ignoring a chirpy hello from Jeffries. 'You should be talking to Imara, not me.'

'I'm talking to you because I know you wouldn't stand by while someone got hurt,' Jana told her, as TJ, Holly and Jeffries got into the back of Becca's car. 'You're human and we trust *you* with the secret, don't we? Doesn't Holly deserve the same chance? Doesn't everyone?'

The scientist shook her head and sighed. 'I shouldn't tell you this,' she said, in a low voice, 'but . . . I made some discreet enquiries about Carrie. I was told that we might not like what we find. My contact heard that Carrie hasn't responded well to treatment. She's being kept heavily sedated to control her violent impulses.'

'Sedated?' Jana repeated. 'How is that "therapy"?'

Doctor Whitewood couldn't answer that. She had a

bigger worry. 'If the girl sees her like that, it could have the opposite effect to the one you're hoping for,' she warned. 'That video will have been seen ten million times by tomorrow morning and we'll be finished at Segolia. In fact, we might be finished full stop.'

Despite Becca's concerns, she did drive them to Carter Hall. It was an imposing place of towers, turrets and high walls made out of solid, carved stone. They pulled up outside an arch in the outer perimeter, beyond which was a neatly clipped lawn that ran right up to the main building.

Doctor Whitewood turned to look at Holly. 'As one fully paid-up Homo sapiens to another: I strongly urge you to let this go.'

Holly shook her head. 'I can't. Carrie needed a friend. That should have been *me*.'

'You two stay in the car,' Jana said to Jeffries and Whitewood. 'No one needs to know you were involved.'

Mr Jeffries actually looked disappointed. 'How are you going to get past the cameras?' he asked.

Jana shrugged, trying to look more confident than she actually felt. 'I'll think of something.'

Jeffries stared at the stone arch for a moment. Then he opened the car door. 'You need a distraction!'

'Sir!' Jana hissed.

'Tim!' called Becca, but Mr Jeffries took no notice of either of them.

'Hello!' the teacher shouted up at the camera. 'Does my

170

National Trust card get me in here for free?' There was no answer. 'English Heritage?' he tried. 'Railcard? Loyalty points?'

The camera swung around to focus on him. Jeffries glanced sideways to see that Jana was making the most of his diversion as she, Holly and TJ scaled the wall out of sight of the camera. Just a few more minutes . . . 'Is there a tea shop, at least?'

There was no answer, but a security guard in a sharp suit appeared on a balcony above him.

'I, er – OK, OK, I'm going,' Jeffries said. 'Right now. Bye!'

He scooted back to the car before the guard had a chance to come down to him.

Jana had brought masks for them to wear. TJ wasn't happy to see that his was, for some reason, a rubber unicorn's head. Still, as Jana pointed out, it beat being caught on CCTV.

They went in through a back door on the ground level that led into a series of small offices. There were neat desks everywhere, all equipped with computers, but the weird thing was that no one was sitting at them. The computers were all on, as if people had been working there just moments before, but now every room was empty. There wasn't a Wolfblood in sight. The place was like the *Marie Celeste*.

171

'Where is everyone?' Jana wondered.

'Who cares?' TJ asked. 'Let's get this done.'

Jana paused before they went on. 'Holly, look,' she said quietly. 'I don't know if she's going to be the Carrie that you knew.'

Holly frowned. 'What?'

'I'm just saying we should be prepared.'

A distraught look passed Holly's face. 'This is on me,' she said brokenly. 'Whatever's happened to her. Because I didn't listen. Because I didn't help her . . .'

'It's not,' said TJ firmly. Jana and Holly looked at him. His face was solemn and guilty. 'I told her I could help her when I couldn't. It's on *me*.'

They found Carrie's room easily – too easily, for Jana's liking. Everywhere was deserted. Something wasn't right. Through the toughened window in the door they could see Carrie, dressed in hospital pyjamas and staring out of the window.

'We need to make this quick,' Jana urged.

'Let me talk to her on my own. Please,' Holly begged. 'Just for a minute.'

Jana nodded. She and TJ stayed outside while Holly went in.

Holly crept closer to her friend, but the girl didn't seem to hear. 'Carrie?' Holly said, scared. She reached out and touched her friend's arm.

172

Carrie turned, slowly, as if she were in a dream. Her face was blank and she stared as if she had no idea who Holly was. Then, slowly, she smiled. The smile didn't reach her eyes, though. Her eyes didn't really seem to show anything at all.

'Holly.'

'Don't worry,' Holly said, shaken. 'Whatever they've done, it stops now. I'll get you out of here.'

Carrie gave that weird smile again. She didn't blink, not even once. 'Holly, I'm not going anywhere,' she said, in a strange, somewhere-else voice. 'I'm fine. Actually I'm better than fine. They've looked after me. They've listened to me and taken care of me and . . . shown me my true self.'

Holly felt her eyes fill with tears. 'The stuff about you being a Wolfblood – it was all true?'

Carrie smiled again. 'It was all true.'

Holly began to cry in earnest then. Carrie hugged her. Holly couldn't help but flinch. After all, this was a creature – a *wolf*. But Carrie held on to her, and it didn't feel like a beast's arms around her. It felt like her friend. Her best friend, whom she had missed *so much* . . . Holly sobbed, finally hugging Carrie back.

'I'm starting a new life, Hol,' Carrie said, in her calm, soothing voice. 'Segolia are going to set me up somewhere no one knows me.'

'But why can't you just come home?' Holly said, struggling to hold back more tears.

173

'There'll be awkward questions,' Carrie told her. 'Things I did that I can't explain away. It's easier like this. You don't have to worry about me. If you're the amazing, brilliant friend that I know you are, you'll forget about us. All of us.'

And that was when the alarm went off. It blared overhead, a loud siren that brought Jana and TJ bursting into the room in panic.

'Time to go!' TJ yelled.

'The window,' Carrie said. 'Go!'

'Come with us,' Holly pleaded as Jana and TJ went.

'You have to go – for me,' Carrie urged. Something flashed through her eyes – something that actually looked like Carrie, just for a moment. 'Now!' she shouted, her voice wild.

TJ and Jana pulled Holly with them, out of the window and away across the grounds. The security guards gave chase, but the younger Wolfbloods had the advantage. They slipped away through the woods to where Jeffries and Whitewood waited with the car.

What none of them saw was Imara heading into Carrie's room. The girl perched on her bed, feeling the well of constant confusion she now lived in swallowing her up again. Had Holly been here? Holly, her old friend? She couldn't really remember now . . .

'You did well, Carrie,' Imara told her, with a warm smile. 'Very well.

174

Carrie looked up at the woman and smiled back. It felt like the right thing to do. It was the right thing to do . . .

Wasn't it?

Seventeen

It was almost full moon, and TJ felt terrible. It was as if he had flu, but the kind a giant would get, not a teenage boy. His teeth hurt; he had a fever. He was miserable. The rest of Segolia were preparing to head off to Scandinavia for their monthly full-moon wolf-out-naturally trip, and TJ just knew he was going to miss it.

'I'm not going to make it to Norway, am I?' he moaned, as his mum stuck a thermometer between his teeth. For some reason, she didn't seem nearly as worried or sympathetic as he thought she should be.

'It looks bad. But you've got to come with us,' she said, checking the thermometer.

'Serious?' TJ said. 'Not like this. Look at me! My ears are supersonic, my teeth ache . . .'

His mum's face took on a stern look. 'Oh yes, *just* like this.' Then her face broke into a wide smile. 'Welcome to the pack, son!'

TJ stared at her as he worked out what she meant. Then he leapt up, so excited he completely forgot how awful he felt. 'I'm going to transform? Really? Is this it?' At his mum's nod he punched the air in triumph.

'Norway here I come! Can. Not. *Wait* to finally give Jana a run for her money!'

'Jana isn't coming this month,' his mum told him. 'She's got a mission.'

TJ stopped dead, crestfallen. 'Mission? What mission? *Where?*'

Jana stared at Doctor Whitewood, who sat in the Kafe with her tablet, waiting for an answer to her question.

'Back to the wild pack?' Jana repeated, stunned.

'I need to see if Meinir's treatment has worked,' Doctor Whitewood explained. 'Are you up for coming with me?'

Jana could barely contain her excitement. 'Just say the word!'

Becca smiled. 'We'll need to be there for her transformation at full moon. Come over when you have a break and we'll make a plan.'

Emilia was desperate for the whole pack to go, but both Jana and Whitewood said no.

'*Why* can't we go?' Emilia asked, hurt. 'We know them. And they know us.'

'Imara would never allow it, even if I asked,' Becca said.

'It'll cause too many problems, Emilia,' said Jana, feeling bad for disappointing the girl. 'For you, your brother, your foster parents. Next time we'll all go. I promise.'

Emilia, obviously upset, got up and went to sit in

another part of the Kafe with Matei and Selina as TJ came in. He was just as upset with Jana as Emilia was, though for a different reason.

'I'm transforming this full moon,' he said shortly.

Jana grinned. 'That's great, TJ!' She went to give him a hug, but he backed away with a frown on his face.

'*You* won't be there.'

'Don't be like that!' Jana tried. 'It's not my fault, is it?' But he just walked past her, going over to talk to Matei and Selina instead.

The only person truly happy that morning was Katrina. 'Ta-da!' she shouted, bursting through the door of the Kafe a few minutes after TJ, brandishing a set of car keys. 'Passed first time!'

Jana smiled, happy for her friend. 'That's brilliant!'

'Will you mind the Kafe for me tomorrow?' Katrina asked. 'I want to take Kay on a spontaneous day out I've been planning for weeks. I know you've got that thing with TJ and his mum, but . . . could you cancel it?'

Jana grimaced. 'Sorry. It's been in the calendar for ages. What about your dad?'

'He's got a big meeting. Come on, Jana, *I'm* more family than they are! What's so important about tomorrow that you can't do another day?'

Jana looked over at Doctor Whitewood, who was busy planning their trip on her tablet. 'Sorry, Katrina. I promised.'

Katina sighed and went off to check on the customers,

starting with Becca. Jana went over to the gang, trying to make amends for their various disappointments. A few minutes later Katrina came over, a steely look in her eyes.

'How come Doctor Whitewood just told me you two were off on some field trip together tomorrow? I thought you said you were going somewhere with TJ and his mum?'

Jana winced. 'Oh. Katrina, sorry, it's just . . .'

Katrina crossed her arms. 'Doctor Whitewood's *still* waiting for her coffee.'

Jana, defeated, went back to the counter as Katrina loomed over TJ.

'What does Jana do for Segolia that's *so* important?' Katrina demanded. 'Where's she going tomorrow? What does your mum *do*, TJ?'

TJ searched for an answer but couldn't find one. 'She just . . . does . . . stuff,' he managed. 'She . . .'

Selina tried to come to his rescue. 'She's probably told him a hundred times, but if there aren't any trainers involved . . .'

Katrina obviously didn't believe a word of it. An awkward silence settled over the table.

'Why don't we follow Jana tomorrow and find out what she does?' Emilia said to Katrina, suddenly. The rest of the Wolfbloods stared at her in horrified shock, but she kept talking before anyone could stop her. 'You've got a car now, haven't you?'

'Yeah,' said Katrina, 'and I was going to take Kay out tomorrow.'

Emilia grinned. 'She can mind the Kafe! Come on, Katrina, you want to know what Jana gets up to? So do we. It's the only way you'll ever find out . . .'

Katrina looked hesitant for a second, and then nodded. 'OK.'

As Katrina headed back to the kitchen, all hell broke loose.

'Are you crazy?' Matei hissed. 'Katrina? The wild pack? Going to the wild pack *with Katrina*? No way. No way!'

Emilia sat back in her chair, sulking. 'I can't face another full moon staring at brick walls. And I want to see Meinir.'

'But *Katrina*?' Matei said again.

'We'll lose her when we get there.'

'And what about Jana?'

'She'll be with her pack.' Emilia shrugged. 'What's not to like?'

'We can't go, they'd spot us following a mile off,' Matei pointed out.

'Use your phone,' TJ suggested. 'You can sync it with Emilia's so you can track it. Put it in Whitewood's car.'

Emilia immediately thrust her phone towards her brother. 'Do it,' she said.

But Matei was all fingers and thumbs, probably because he didn't really want to make it work in the first place. In the end TJ grabbed both phones and sorted out the app and the sync for him. Then he got up and went for the door, sneaking Doctor Whitewood's car keys from the table as he passed.

Within minutes TJ was back in the Kafe, having stashed Emilia's phone under the driver's seat of Doctor Whitewood's car. He gave the scientist her keys back as he passed.

'You must have accidentally kicked these under the table,' he said as he handed them to her, smooth as you like. He slid back into his seat opposite Matei and said, 'Check your phone.'

Matei opened the Find My Fone app on his screen. There was a red dot blinking on the map – Emilia's phone. They were in business.

'Guess we really are going,' Matei muttered.

Emilia grinned. 'Awesome, TJ!'

Selina put her hands over her ears in mock-horror. 'Oh, I do not want to hear this!'

Emilia, beaming, threw a high five at TJ and said, 'Why don't you swap Norway for us?'

TJ stared at her. It was a very, very tempting thought.

Despite the upset it had caused with her friends, Jana couldn't wait to get back to the wild. Sure, it was only a visit, but it had been too long since she'd seen her wild pack – her true family. The next morning she was up before dawn, dressed in her wild gear and ready to go. She crept out to avoid waking Katrina, slipping down the stairs and out of the flat to find Doctor Whitewood already waiting for her.

The further Jana got from the city, the wilder she felt. She watched out of the window as the buildings grew further apart, as the gardens of the houses they passed grew larger and larger before eventually turning into fields. Still they drove, mostly in silence, as the terrain grew ever wilder, more rugged and mountainous.

The only sound that broke the silence was the ringing of Whitewood's phone. The doctor flicked on the loud-speaker.

'Hello?'

'Is TJ with you?' It was Imara's voice at her most stern, booming into the quiet car.

Jana and Doctor Whitewood looked at each other, frowning. 'TJ?' Jana said. 'No.'

'Are you sure? He's not answering his phone.'

'Imara, I can assure you he's not here,' said Becca. 'Is there anything we can help with?'

'No,' the Segolia alpha said shortly. 'Just give me a status report as soon as you have something.' She hung up abruptly.

'What's TJ up to?' Jana wondered.

Eighteen

At that moment, TJ was with Matei and Emilia in Katrina's extremely pink car, trying to ignore his phone ringing with yet another call as they bombed along some distance behind Doctor Whitewood's four-wheel drive. He'd decided to join this crazy expedition at the last minute, and he was beginning to realise just what a massive mistake he'd made.

'Your mum again?' Matei asked.

'That was Jana. Mum must have called her . . .' TJ gritted his teeth as Matei winced. They both knew he was going to be in *so much* trouble for this.

'This is the life!' Katrina said breezily, completely oblivious. She took a deep breath, and then almost choked as the odour of manure clogged up her nose. She recovered and sighed happily. 'Ahh, those country *smells*!' She wound up her window. 'How about a game of I Spy?' she suggested.

TJ, Emilia and Matei stifled a collective sigh. It was going to be a long day.

Jana and Doctor Whitewood drove for hours. They went so far and into terrain that was so remote that the SatNav gave up completely. It just couldn't get a signal.

'Still no chance of any coordinates?' Becca asked Jana, again, as the road turned into more of a dirt track.

'Don't need them,' Jana said, smiling out of the window with a dreamy look on her face.

'I'd love to run some tests,' the scientist said, looking over at her. 'Find out more about that innate sense of location and direction you have.'

'Why does everything have to have a scientific explanation?' asked Jana, shaking her head. 'Can't things just *be*?'

'I can tell you're getting closer to home,' Becca laughed. 'You're sounding like a wild again! We are nearly there, though, aren't we?' the scientist asked. '*My* senses tell me: negative population density, increased flora and foliage and no infrastructure –'

Jana frowned. 'Infrastructure?'

'We've run out of road,' Whitewood pointed out, as even the dirt path disappeared into the dense forest around them and she was forced to stop the car.

'Yes,' said Jana. 'We're nearly there.'

They got out and took their kit out of the car – a rucksack for both of them, and additional scientific equipment for Doctor Whitewood's tests. Becca looked at the landscape. The sun was already dipping low in the sky.

'How long until we arrive?' she asked Jana, as they struck out into the wilderness.

'Not long,' Jana replied, still in that dreamy tone of voice.

Becca was relieved. She wasn't sure how far she could walk with all this equipment. Half an hour would probably be her maximum.

'Only about another three hours,' Jana added, almost as an afterthought.

Katrina had pulled over at a crossroads so that she could have a quick pit stop. TJ, Matei and Emilia took the opportunity to stretch their cramped legs and try to come up with a plan of action, because this wasn't going quite as they'd imagined.

'Who knew Katrina would be so . . . determined?' TJ muttered. 'How are we going to send her home?'

Emilia at least had the good grace to look guilty.

'Relax,' Matei said reassuringly. 'If the trauma of weeing behind a bush doesn't send her running back to the city, nothing will!'

Katrina chose that moment to reappear, looking a little awkward and embarrassed.

'All right, Katrina?' Matei asked. 'Bearing up?'

Katrina surprised them all by squaring her shoulders. 'I'm made of stern stuff, me,' she declared. 'Onwards, Team Kafe!'

'Team . . . *Kafe*?' TJ repeated in dismay. He looked at Matei and Emilia. It really didn't seem as if Katrina was showing any intention of giving up.

Their problems only intensified when they realised they were catching up with Whitewood's car. Emilia's phone had stopped moving sometime before – they had clearly parked somewhere. It wasn't long until the stationary 4x4 loomed into view, parked at the end of a dirt track. There was no sign of Jana or Whitewood. Katrina pulled up, sounding cheerful.

'Fantastic! The end is nigh!' she said, happily, as she climbed out. 'Come on, all of you! Chop, chop!'

'Katrina?' TJ ventured, as their driver began to prepare to hike off into the wild. 'It's taken half a day to get here, we don't know where we are, where *they* are, how far they've walked . . . Let's just call it quits.'

Emilia grabbed his arm. 'What are you *doing*?' she whispered.

TJ whispered back, keeping his eye on Katrina. 'At this rate, we won't get anywhere until after dark and, hello, *newsflash*!' He pulled back his sleeve, showing the black veins already showing on his arms. 'I'm transforming tonight!'

That finally seemed to get through to both Emilia and Matei. TJ raised his voice again, calling after Katrina as she walked off. 'Katrina! We *have* to go back!'

186

'No way!' Katrina called back. 'There's fresh foot-prints here. We'll track them! We're heading out. I'm out-Grylling Bear Grylls!' She marched away as the others looked on in horror.

'We didn't think this through, did we?' Emilia whis-pered.

'We! *We?*' Matei hissed. 'This was *your* idea!'

'I thought she'd give up when she got bored,' said Emilia. 'Don't worry, we'll think of something. The wild pack is probably miles away. Katrina's bound to get tired and want to come back. Won't she?'

TJ wasn't convinced. 'I'm calling Jana,' he said, pulling out his phone. But he had no signal. 'Oh no,' he said, as a feeling of dread crept over him. They had no choice but to follow Katrina, even as the sun continued to drop slowly towards the horizon.

The wild Wolfbloods were hard at work. There were pelts to be cured and stretched, there was hunting and gathering to be done. The coming full moon had made them all restless, and when Jana's scent floated to them on the breeze, added excitement flooded through the makeshift camp.

Jana arrived to find her pack gathered and waiting for her. Aran stood in front of them all, the cubs Cadwr and Gwyn just behind him. He bowed, deeply, and the rest followed suit, the gesture rippling through the assembled

Wolfbloods like a wave. Whitewood stood back, miles outside her comfort zone as Jana accepted the gesture.

But although Jana smiled, her eyes searched the pack and did not find what she was looking for. Anxiety flooded over her. Something wasn't right here. The bow ended. Aran stepped forward and the cubs hugged Jana tightly.

'Where is my father?' Jana wanted to know.

Aran's face betrayed his anxiety. 'Jana . . . I –'

A terrible feeling of cold flooded through her and Jana ran, dashing through the camp to her father's tent. Alric's abode was the biggest, set in the centre as an alpha's home should be. But it was quiet. *Too* quiet. Jana pushed her way in to find her father lying prone on the ground. She gasped as she took in his yellow skin and thin, exhausted face. Kneeling beside him was a Wolfblood she didn't recognise, dressed in the traditional skins of a healer. But all Jana cared about was her father.

'Dad!' She stepped further into the tent as Aran and Doctor Whitewood followed.

Alric opened his eyes and tried to smile. 'Jana . . . I knew you'd come.'

Jana dropped to her knees, wrapping her arms around him. 'What's wrong? Dad?'

Alric put his weak arms around her. 'Jana,' he said, in barely a whisper. 'This full moon . . . it will be my last. I'm dying.'

'No,' Jana sobbed, heartbroken.

188

'You're not dying,' said the strange Wolfblood beside them. 'Not while I have breath in my body.'

'This is Madoc,' Alric breathed. 'We took him in. He lost his pack to . . .'

'Humans,' Madoc finished, casting a hard look at Doctor Whitewood. 'I lost my pack to humans.' He gave Jana the same look. 'The daughter of Alric. It is an honour to meet you. The Wolfblood who walks in both worlds . . . and who has brought some of that world to this.'

'The human my daughter has brought is a healer,' Alric said quietly.

'A healer?' Madoc scoffed. 'But our history tells us humans only know how to destroy. And when one comes, another follows. And another, and another – until there is nowhere left for us.'

'I promise,' said Jana. 'It's just me and Doctor Whitewood here now.'

'I trust my daughter,' Alric said, as firmly as he could. 'And Doctor Whitewood helped all of us escape from the madman who wanted us gone.'

'All humans are mad,' observed Madoc. 'But, if Alric trusts . . . then I trust, too.'

'I'm here for Meinir,' said Becca. 'Where is she?'

Jana looked up from her father as silence fell on the tent. She could tell that Aran was upset, even though he tried to hide it.

'The wolf in her faded,' rasped Alric.

'When Ceri and Gerwyn came to say goodbye, she chose to go with them to start a new life elsewhere,' Aran added. 'We . . . we don't know where.'

'What do you think they're doing out here?' Katrina asked, as she continued to march – or at least to stumble – enthusiastically onwards.

TJ shrugged. 'Collecting medicinal plants?' he suggested. He turned to Matei and Emilia, who were lagging behind. 'If anyone's got any ideas about how we get out of this mess,' he whispered, 'now would be a good time!'

'We've got to leave her,' Emilia whispered back. 'She can find her way back to the car.'

'We can't just ditch her!' TJ hissed, watching as Katrina stumbled and tripped her way forward. 'She'll get lost! We can't do that to her. Emilia – this is on *you*.'

Matei shook his head. 'If she says "Team Kafe" one more time . . .'

'Ow!' Katrina said, as she turned her ankle against a tree root, but still continued to hobble forward. 'Come on, Team Kafe!' she urged.

With no other choice, the Wolfbloods went on. The sun sank towards evening, and TJ could feel his blood fizzing in his veins. This should be the best night of his life, but here he was, stuck in the middle of nowhere with a bunch of idiots. What had he been thinking?

'We're going the wrong way,' he said, a little later.

190

'How do you know?' Katrina asked, leaning on him as her ankle got worse.

'I just do,' he muttered, throwing Matei and Emilia a look and changing direction.

Jana glanced up as Madoc suddenly froze. Outside the tent, she could hear the wild Wolfbloods begin to snarl.

'Someone's coming,' growled Madoc, staring at Jana as if his eyes could slice her in two.

Jana breathed deeply and caught a scent she recognised. It smelled like . . . Oh no – surely it couldn't be . . . *Katrina?*

'You promised your father it was just you and the "healer",' Madoc snarled, as the wild Wolfbloods grew more and more agitated. 'I smell another human!'

'Jana?' Alric asked.

Jana didn't know what to say. She was too shocked. Madoc didn't wait for her to speak. He was already veining up, ready to transform. He stalked out of the tent, and Jana went to follow him.

'Jana?' Alric asked. 'What is happening?'

She looked at her father, too weak to even move, wanting to stay with him – but she knew her friends needed her more. 'I'll come straight back,' she said. 'Stay with Doctor Whitewood.'

By the time she got outside, the wild Wolfbloods were rushing into the woods, ready for the hunt.

* * *

Around them, the forest had closed in as the evening drew on. It was almost as if there was nothing in the world any more but trees.

'We're lost, aren't we?' Katrina said, now hobbling so badly that she couldn't walk at all without TJ's help.

TJ sniffed, panic rising through him as he realised the scent of the wild Wolfbloods was growing closer.

'It's worse than that,' he muttered.

A second later the trees were full of snarling, rushing Wolfbloods. They poured out of the looming darkness, still in human form, but all yellow eyes and ferocious bared teeth.

Katrina screamed at the sight of them, almost falling over as TJ pushed her back behind him. Matei and Emilia crowded in, instinctively veining up themselves.

Then Jana appeared. She leapt clean over the milling, snarling wild Wolfbloods, landing in front of her friends and spinning to face the wild pack.

Katrina clung to TJ, but when she looked at his face, she realised he was like the others – his eyes were yellow and his teeth were bared. He was growling, snarling like a wild animal . . . She tried to move away, but then she realised that Emilia and Matei were exactly the same!

'Jana!' Katrina screamed, absolutely petrified. 'Help me!'

Jana turned to look at her. The last thing Katrina saw

before she collapsed completely was that her flatmate's eyes were glowing yellow and her teeth were bared. Then she fainted clean away.

TJ, Emilia and Matei stood beside Jana. She was defiant, strong, facing off against the wild pack. Behind them was Madoc, staring at her angrily.

'*Bradwr.*'

The word whispered around the pack, growing louder each time another Wolfblood said it.

'*Bradwr. Bradwr. BRADWR!*'

Jana knew exactly what it meant.

Traitor.

Nineteen

The wild Wolfbloods began to close in, snarling.

'Enough!' shouted a weak voice.

It was Alric. He was being helped through the woods by Aran. Silence fell as the wild pack backed away, bowing to their alpha.

'I told you not to come here!' Jana hissed to the city Wolfbloods, as their wolves subsided, too. 'This isn't a game!'

'We're sorry,' Emilia said, shaken.

Alric approached Jana. 'They're my pack,' she told him. 'They have disobeyed me and followed from the city. I'm sorry.'

There was a weak moan as Katrina came around. 'Jana . . .'

Jana turned to look at her friend. 'Don't worry,' she said. 'I won't let anything happen to you.'

Alric turned on the wild pack, furious. 'These are young cubs, still finding their way. They are my daughter's pack. You harm them, you harm me.' The wilds retreated as Alric turned back to Jana with a proud yet serious look on his face. 'If Madoc can't help me,' he said, 'I want you to take my place. To lead my pack. This is my last wish.'

Jana stared at him in shock as his words sank in.

Alric, Jana and Aran led the two packs back into camp, where Doctor Whitewood waited with Cadwr and Gwyn.

'We've got some uninvited guests,' Jana told the stunned-looking scientist as TJ, Matei, Emilia and Katrina arrived.

When the cubs saw Emilia, they were fascinated. They ran up to her with wide eyes, staring at her scars.

'Touched by fire,' they both whispered.

'Aran and Meinir told us about you,' Gwyn said.

'We've never seen a wolf that's walked through fire,' Cadwr added.

Emilia nodded to Matei. 'We both did. My brother carried me through it. He saved my life.'

The cubs stared at Matei, awestruck.

'Show our guests around the camp,' Aran told the cubs, and they scampered off with Emilia and Matei following behind.

TJ helped Katrina to a log. 'I know, I know,' he said to Doctor Whitewood, who was staring daggers at him. 'Mum's going to kill me.'

'TJ,' said the scientist, 'Imara may be your mum, but she's my *boss*. This is serious. You have no idea . . .'

Whitewood trailed off, but TJ could tell that she was genuinely worried. That scared him, in turn. Was his

195

mum really that bad? She couldn't be, could she? She was his mum.

'Are you here to fix these people?' Katrina asked the scientist. 'What's with the eyes? The teeth? Is – is what they've got catching?'

Becca glanced at Katrina's ankle. 'No. I'll give you some painkillers for your ankle.'

Before she could move, Madoc loomed over them. His face wasn't friendly, but at least he wasn't growling. 'It is against my better judgement, but I will apply a balm,' he told Katrina. 'It will diminish the swelling and heal.'

'Doctor Whitewood!'

It was Jana, calling Becca to her father's tent. The scientist went to see what she wanted, Madoc hurrying after them as soon as he'd dealt with Katrina's ankle.

Inside, Jana knelt beside her father, Aran on the other side of him. Alric took Jana's hand and then Aran's, too.

'Doctor Whitewood,' she said, as Becca arrived. 'Please help him . . .'

But Madoc pushed past the human doctor, picking up a bowl of wild Wolfblood potion and kneeling beside Alric.

Alric squeezed Jana's hand. 'Jana, if I am to be healed, it will be by Madoc's hand. Every alpha must trust in their healer. It is our way. You know that.'

Jana was on the verge of tears. Becca put a hand on her shoulder and peered into Madoc's bowl. 'Could I

take a sample?' she asked. 'Ceri told me these old remedies are more potent than our medicines.'

Madoc didn't even look at her. 'Did she not also tell
you these remedies are a pack secret?'

'Yes, but . . .'

'Then you'll know that we do not share our healing
with humans,' the Wolfblood healer said shortly.

'Leave us,' Alric said to the room. 'I must speak with
Jana. Alone.'

Aran and Doctor Whitewood made their way out of
the tent, but Madoc stayed put. He smiled at Jana. 'I
am trusted,' he said. 'Your father's life is my life.'

Alric nodded. 'Jana,' he began softly. 'Aran's been lost
without Meinir. Now he is found: the alpha he was always
meant to be. I want you to rule – with Aran by your side.'

Jana stared at him. Aran? As her mate? She'd never
once thought of him that way. Whenever she thought of
a potential mate, another face loomed in her mind.
Matei . . . She pushed that away, her cheeks flushing hot.

'Father, Aran and me, I . . . can't . . .' she began. Alric
turned away, a disapproving look on his face. 'You'll be
better soon anyway. Won't he?' Jana asked Madoc.

Madoc looked up from his potion. 'Yes, all better
soon. Drink,' he told Alric, holding the bowl to his
alpha's lips. Then he looked up. 'The full moon is soon
upon us. We must gather.'

* * *

197

Jana, TJ, Matei and Emilia followed the wild Wolfbloods as Madoc led them to a clearing just outside the camp. The moon was huge where it hung in the pitch-black sky overhead. TJ could feel the fizz of his wolf in his veins, stronger than ever before. It was under his skin, just waiting to get out – and this time, it actually would. He couldn't wait. Finally he'd be like his friends. Finally he'd be able to really understand what it meant to be a Wolfblood.

'Form a circle,' Madoc said, his voice hushed and reverent. 'Join hands . . .'

Madoc began to speak as the circle joined hands one by one.

'Feel the power of the moon as it flows in our blood,' said the healer, his words almost like a chant, 'and pushes us and pulls us like the tides . . .'

Matei reached for Jana's hand, but Aran beat him to it.

'. . . its light shows us the way . . .' Madoc went on, '. . . and gives us strength and guides us . . . . From our first transformation to our last . . .'

'I feel amazing!' TJ whispered. 'Like . . . like nothing else in the world!'

Emilia grinned, feeling it too, staring up at the sky, at the huge, huge moon.

A little distance away, Katrina and Doctor Whitewood sat together, watching. Katrina couldn't really see what was going on, but whatever it was, it was well weird.

'What's happening?' she asked Becca, who had her scientific notebook out and was frantically scribbling notes into it.

'Something incredible,' the scientist told her. 'There's nothing I can say, Katrina, except: brace yourself!'

Katrina wasn't sure she liked the sound of that. In fact, she was beginning to think that coming here at all had been a very bad idea. Katrina got out her phone, wondering if she should call her dad, but she still had no signal. She bit her lip, feeling sick. Anything could happen to her out here, and no one back home would ever know. She thought for another second and flicked on the video, holding it up so she could film herself.

'To whoever finds this, I'm stuck in the middle of nowhere with Jana's weird cult,' Katrina began. 'They're all holding hands. I think they're witches. I think they . . . they . . .'

Sounds began to come from the circle of people. Katrina looked up. They were all quivering as if they had been electrified. They shook, throwing their heads back to look at the moon, making strange yipping and snarling noises. She could tell something was going to happen. Something huge . . . Without even thinking, Katrina turned the camera around and began to film.

What she saw was terrifying.

The people in the circle began to change. Their eyes

turned yellow again, and strange threads of black blood traced through their veins.

Then there weren't people in the circle any more.

They were . . .

They were . . .

Katrina didn't even have words to describe it. She backed away, continuing to film, even though every part of her was shaking like a leaf.

Wolves. That what her friends had turned into. Wolves!

Twenty

Calm descended as the sun rose the next morning. Becca was sitting in Alric's tent. Beside her, Katrina lay on the Wolfblood alpha's blanket, still asleep. She had been terrified the night before, and Becca could understand that. Finding out about Wolfbloods was enough to take in all on its own. Discovering the secret by seeing an entire wild pack transform at once – she probably would have freaked out a little bit herself if she'd been in Katrina's shoes.

Alric walked into the tent, followed by Jana. Their footsteps roused Katrina, who jerked awake and then leapt up with a little scream.

'You don't need to be scared,' Jana told her, as Katrina backed away.

'Scared?' Katrina said defiantly. 'I'm furious! You've lied to me for, like, *ever*! Since Stoneybridge. All those times – wolves in the woods, it was *you*!'

'We mean you no harm,' Alric said quietly, sitting as his legs threatened to give way.

'I know it's a lot to take in,' Jana told Katrina. 'I'll answer any questions you have. But my father's ill. Doctor Whitewood? Will you please look at him?'

Madoc appeared. 'Do not touch him,' the Wolfblood healer warned, fussing around his alpha. 'He'll soon be back to his best. He must rest. Leave us!'

Becca gathered her things. Katrina gripped her arm, refusing to let go as they made their way out of the tent with Jana behind them.

The others were waiting with Aran as Jana appeared. 'How is your father?' Aran asked.

Jana couldn't speak, so she just shook her head. Aran tried to comfort her, but she shook him away.

'Right,' said Katrina decisively. 'Back to the car and back to the Kafe. We'll call your dad an ambulance.'

'The nearest hospital is a hundred miles way. And you don't call anyone,' Jana told her. 'Doctor Whitewood – Dad won't let you treat him here. If I try to persuade him to come with us, will you wait?'

'Of course,' Becca told her. 'I'd like to explore the area anyway, collect some samples.'

'The rest of you, go home,' Jana told her pack. 'There's nothing keeping you here. And, Katrina, what you've seen here – it stays between us.' She went back into her father's tent, leaving the rest of them staring after her.

'Well, I'm not going,' Emilia said. The others all turned to stare at her, but she just shrugged.

'We have to,' said Katrina. 'My dad'll be frantic!'

'And Mum's going to *murder* me,' TJ added.

Emilia crossed her arms, determined. 'Jana's our alpha. She stays, we stay.'

Matei looked at his little sister for a moment, and then nodded. 'She might need us,' he pointed out to TJ.

'I know, I know,' TJ sighed. 'Jana's our alpha. She leads, we follow.'

'And she *told* us to go,' Katrina pointed out. 'Tell them, Doctor Whitewood!' Katrina followed as Becca headed for her kit.

'Sorry,' Whitewood told her. 'I've got research to do while I'm here. This is a once-in-a-lifetime opportunity for me.'

'What?' Katrina said, flabbergasted, as Becca calmly headed into the woods. 'You can't leave me with these . . . *things*!'

'I heard that,' said TJ's voice, behind Katrina. 'We aren't *things*. We're Wolfbloods. Want to hear all about us?'

Katrina looked at him doubtfully. Then she nodded.

Jana couldn't persuade her father to come with her back to Segolia. Or rather, she couldn't persuade Madoc to let him go. She picked up one of the healer's bowls, sniffing it and grimacing.

'This smells like nothing Ceri ever made,' she said.

'I have been doing this far longer than Ceri,' Madoc

told her. 'I carry a thousand years of knowledge in me. Like my father and his father's father going back to when the world was young and we stood proud in the world with our kin. The same wolves humans have hunted to extinction.' Madoc shook his head. 'You've been too long in their world. You've gone tame. You worry and weaken your father. The best thing you can do for him is to go, leave this place.'

'I'm not leaving him,' Jana said, firmly.

'Humans weaken us, they always have. And you? You reek of them. What are you? Human or wolf?'

Jana raised her chin and looked at him. 'I'm my father's daughter.'

Madoc nodded, seeming pleased. 'Then assist me.' He pointed to the bowl she'd turned her nose up at. 'Give it to your father. I must go, make some more.'

'Jana,' Alric said. 'Trust Madoc. He is wise and true.'

If her father trusted Madoc, who was she to argue? Jana knelt beside her father and held the bowl to his lips as Madoc gathered his equipment and left.

It felt wrong to Jana, nursing her father like this. She remembered how, as a young cub, she'd thought Alric must be the strongest Wolfblood in the world. Now all she wanted was for him to survive. The thought filled her heart with a pain so great she could hardly bear it. Once her father fell asleep, she crept out of the tent and found a quiet spot near the edge of camp. She just wanted to be on her own for a while, but Aran came to find her. He meant well, but she couldn't help but tense up when he laid a hand on her shoulder. Especially now she knew how Aran fitted into her father's wishes.

'We must talk,' Aran said quietly. 'About the pack. About who should lead.'

Jana looked away. 'I'm not thinking about that. Ever.'

Aran was silent for a while and then he said, '*We* should lead. Together. You and me.'

Jana swallowed. 'You can lead. *If* the time comes.'

'Not without you,' he said softly.

'Aran. You're like a brother to me.' Jana stood up. 'I can't! I just . . . can't!'

She left him sitting there alone, and couldn't even bring herself to look back.

Cadwr and Gwyn had decided to show Emilia and Matei more of their camp. They took them to the storage tent. Inside were all the pelts the pack had cured, the baskets they had made, their hunting weapons, the dyes they used on their clothes. Emilia stared around in wonder.

'Do you make *all* this?' she asked in wonder.

Gwyn nodded proudly. 'From what we find or catch.'

'It's amazing,' she breathed. Even Matei seemed impressed.

Cadwr pulled out a net. 'Do you two want to come hunting with me?'

'I ought to stay close to Jana,' said Matei, not quite looking Emilia in the eye as he said it.

Emilia nodded. She understood. She hoped Jana knew how lucky she was to have Matei care for her so much.

'I'd love to come,' she told Cadwr.

Cadwr took her out of the camp and into the forest beyond. 'You walk like a *human*,' he said with faint disgust, after listening to her footsteps for a while.

'No, I don't!' Emilia protested. 'Do I?'

'You must walk like the wild wood, *look* like the wild wood, *smell* like the wild wood,' Cadwr told her, before grabbing a handful of mossy earth and rubbing it all over his face and body.

'Seriously?' Emilia asked, watching.

'Slow your heart, your breath,' Cadwr said quietly. '*Be* the wild wood . . .' As she watched, Cadwr stepped into the bushes. A second later he had vanished. Emilia sniffed, trying to get his scent – but he'd gone. Completely gone. Then, just as swiftly, he reappeared in front of her.

She gasped. 'Teach me!'

But Cadwr shook his head. 'No. You can't learn. It is in your heart or it's not.'

The young Wolfblood reached out and smeared a line of earth across her forehead and down her nose, and then pointed deep into the woods.

'Go and see,' he told her.

Emilia was nervous about the idea of going into the

206

forest alone, but she wanted to learn all the wild ways that she could. She'd never felt at home in the human world. Here, she felt as if she could fit in, properly, if only she could be like Cadwr.

She crept through the trees. The further into the forest she got, the more Emilia felt a part of everything around her. Up ahead, she heard a sound – someone singing. She crept forward, over the crest of a wooded hill thick with lush undergrowth. Below her she could see Madoc the healer moving slowly along a path thick with fallen leaves. He carried a basket, and every now and then he stopped to pick a plant or two. Emilia crouched behind a trunk, trying to blend into the wild wood the way Cadwr had.

Madoc froze suddenly and turned sharply, as if he'd scented her. Emilia held her breath – she was right in front of him! But after a moment it was obvious he couldn't see her. She smiled – she'd done it! She *could* be a wild Wolfblood.

'Boo!' she said, stepping out of the foliage right in front of Madoc.

He narrowed his dark eyes at her for a second. 'You have learned much in the short time you've been here.'

'I have!' Emilia smiled back. 'Are you gathering your medicines to cure Alric?

'Yes . . . yes,' he told her, with a slow smile. 'Comfrey for fever, mandrake for restfulness . . .'

'Emilia!' called a voice from the forest behind them.

It was Doctor Whitewood, carrying some sample boxes. She smiled as she came closer.

'Madoc,' she said. 'I know your traditions. But we are both healers. Perhaps we could share our knowledge?'

Madoc scowled at the human woman with utter disdain. 'Healer? When I look at you, all I see are the ghosts of wolves who will never howl again.'

Whitewood looked shocked and Emilia tried to break the tension. 'It's comfrey and mandrake,' she said helpfully.

But Becca frowned as she glanced at the plants in Madoc's basket. He tried to hide them away.

'That doesn't look like comfrey . . .' she said. Her eyes flashed to Madoc's in shock. 'This is hemlock! It's poisonous!'

Madoc snarled suddenly, his eyes yellowing. Becca swallowed, moving slightly so that she stood in front of Emilia.

'Emilia,' she said, more calmly than she felt. 'Go back to camp.'

Madoc moved in, his eyes still showing the yellow of his wolf-self. 'Come here, child,' he said to Emilia. 'Come away from the human.'

Emilia stayed behind Doctor Whitewood, her heart pounding as she watched Madoc grow angrier. The healer moved forward and Becca and Emilia backed away. They left the path, stepping onto rougher ground, brambles and tree roots tangling around their ankles with every small step they took.

'You have corrupted this poor cub,' Madoc barked. 'Look at her – burned, twisted. Human!'

'I'm a Wolfblood!' Emilia snarled.

'Silence!' Madoc snarled back, moving ever forward as Doctor Whitewood and Emilia continued to stumble backwards, deeper into the undergrowth. 'When you forsake wolves for humans, you miss out on our strengths, our traditions. Our history. Our *stories*!'

Becca glanced down and saw with shock that without them realising it, Madoc had pushed them to the edge of a rocky cliff that plunged down into a deep ravine.

'Do you know . . .' Madoc went on, slowly, 'what happened to the curious little cub?' His yellow eyes were glowing with fury, fixed on Emilia's face as he moved closer.

There was a sliver of silence as Emilia stared back, silent and open-mouthed.

'*NOBODY DOES!*' Madoc bellowed.

His sudden yell made them both jump. Emilia shrieked and slid over the cliff with Doctor Whitewood crashing down beside her. They both scrabbled desperately for something to hold on to, clinging to the ground beneath their fingers as they hung over the deep drop below.

'Help us!' Whitewood shouted as Madoc looked down at them.

He smiled slowly and then walked away, still carrying his poisonous herbs.

Matei was sitting with TJ and Katrina when he looked up and saw Cadwr walking past. The cub was alone, though – there was no sign of Emilia. Matei stood up and stopped the youngster with a frown.

'Where's my sister?' he asked.

Cadwr nodded over his shoulder to the trees. 'In the forest.'

'What? Alone?' Matei said, feeling a tight knot of worry start to form in his stomach.

Cadwr shrugged. 'It's better that way,' he said.

Matei wasn't so sure. Emilia wasn't like the wild Wolfblood cubs. She'd only ever known the city, and she'd always had him there to look after her. He sniffed, searching for his sister's scent, but he couldn't pick it up – not here, surrounded by the wild pack. Matei headed into the forest, still sniffing, his heart pounding heavily. Where was she?

Inside her father's tent, Jana was becoming frantic. No matter how much of Madoc's potion Jana made Alric drink, he just kept getting sicker and sicker.

'Please don't leave me,' she begged him, in tears as he faded further and further away from the living. 'Don't die!' She looked around as Madoc came in.

'Quick,' the healer told her, dumping the herbs he'd gathered into his pestle and mortar and handing it to her. 'Mix these. Quickly!'

'Jana,' he said, a moment later. 'Your father talked of me leading the pack if anything happened to him. Just for a short time. Until you and Aran . . . are ready. It is for the best. For the pack. For you. Yes?'

Jana was so focused on mixing the medicine that she barely listened to what he was saying. She just nodded, still mixing.

'Good.' Madoc smiled. 'Keep mixing, then give it to your father. I will gather the pack.'

He left and Jana carried on stirring for a few minutes. Then she threw down the bowl, realising that this was hopeless. Unless . . .

'I don't care about tradition,' she sobbed, standing up. 'I'm getting Doctor Whitewood!'

She ran from the tent and followed Doctor Whitewood's trail into the woods. Ahead of her she caught a familiar scent, and realised it was Matei. She could sense that Emilia and the scientist were with him – but something was wrong. Very, *very* wrong.

She could smell their fear. The scent permeated the air – but no, it wasn't just fear. It was worse than that, sharper, sicker.

Jana raced through the undergrowth, dodging and weaving, the scent of pure terror washing towards her through the greenery. Then there was a sharp, piercing scream – Emilia!

She reached the clearing just in time to see Matei hanging over the edge of the cliff as if he were clinging to something. He was slipping, his feet scrabbling against the soft ground . . .

Jana leapt forward and saw that below him, right over a deep ravine, hung Emilia. Jana flung herself down and only just managed to catch hold of Doctor Whitewood before she slipped away entirely. Jana held on to her with every ounce of strength she had.

'Climb!' Jana urged Becca as she and Matei began to pull her and Emilia both up. 'Climb, now!'

Together she and Matei managed to haul both of them back up and over the edge into the clearing. They all lay in a heap, relieved and exhausted.

'Madoc,' Whitewood gasped, once she'd managed to regain her breath. 'It was *Madoc*!'

The healer had ordered the entire wild pack to gather, and no one ever disobeyed Madoc. It was understood that he was to be as respected as Alric himself. It would usually only be an alpha that called such a meeting, but there was no sign of their sick leader – or of Jana. One by one, the wild Wolfbloods hesitantly left what they were doing and formed an uncertain circle outside Alric's tent, looking at one another. Aran

212

stood in front of Madoc, wondering what was going on.

'Alric,' Madoc began, his voice booming through the quiet forest, 'has passed leadership of the pack . . . to *me*.'

A ripple of whispers ran through the gathered Wolfbloods.

'Jana has already agreed,' Madoc told them, sensing doubt.

'No!' shouted Aran, shocked. 'Jana would never –'

Madoc snarled at him. 'Jana has already agreed,' he insisted. 'In front of her *father*.'

Aran backed away a step, stunned as he tried to take in the healer's words. Surely Jana would not have done this? Not without at least speaking to him first?

'Look at him,' Madoc sneered, taking advantage of Aran's confusion and calling it weakness. 'Not even half a wolf now. No one supports you. No one wants you. Know your place!'

Aran backed away, his head down.

'Swear allegiance to *me*!' Madoc commanded the pack.

TJ got up from where he was sitting with Katrina, motioning for her to stay put. He went to stand with Aran. If there were sides to be taken here, he wanted everyone to be very sure where he stood. That would always be with Jana. Tension among the confused pack began to build. The Wolfbloods were restless, pacing this way and that, unsure what to do. Their wolves were rising to the surface, eyes yellowing, veins blackening.

'Now!' Madoc shouted, again. '*Swear!*'

The pack looked to Aran, but he kept his head down. They had to have a leader, and if Alric had said that it should be Madoc . . . they must obey their alpha's final wish. As one, they prepared to offer the Wolfblood bow.

'Stop!' shouted a voice.

It was Jana. She strode into the gathering, her head held high and her eyes angry.

'He is poisoning my father!' she told the pack, pointing at Madoc.

'Lies!' Madoc cried. 'From the mouth of a tame more human than wolf!'

Jana threw down the poisonous herb shown her by Doctor Whitewood. 'This is hemlock! *This* is what he has been giving to my father!'

The pack turned to Madoc, confused and suspicious. Together they began to growl, showing their teeth.

'You traitor!' Aran growled, looking at Madoc. 'Alric's illness began after *you* arrived.'

At first Madoc tried to resist them. He growled and bared his teeth, but the pack was united now, standing behind Jana and Aran. Madoc transformed, snarling, his wolf full of fury at being denied the leadership of this pack. But then he realised that the entire pack was ready to leap on him at any moment. Not even the strongest wolf would survive that kind of confrontation. Madoc

214

backed away, still growling. Then he turned tail and fled into the forest.

'Leave him!' Jana commanded, before any of them could follow. 'He won't be back.'

Alric began to recover as soon as Doctor Whitewood treated him. He was already able to stand for longer periods, and he was there with the rest of the wild pack when they gathered to say goodbye to the city-dwellers and their human friends.

'It will take a few days to clean the toxins out of you,' Becca told Alric. 'The medicine I've given you will help.'

Alric nodded a thank you and then looked at Jana. 'Will you stay?' he asked.

Jana shook her head. 'I can't. There's something more for me, back in the city. I feel it calling. I have to go back.'

Alric smiled. 'Our packs are joined now. You are always welcome here,' he said, as they hugged. 'I am proud of you, Jana. You are destined for something beyond the wild wood and the city. I feel it.'

As they finally prepared to leave, though, Emilia dropped a bombshell.

'I'm not going,' she told Matei. 'I want to stay here.'

'What?' Matei exploded. 'What are you on about? Madoc just tried to kill you!'

'But he didn't. I'm part of this place.' Emilia said. 'It's in my heart. It's where I belong.'

'What about *my* heart?' Matei asked, taking his sister's hand.

Emilia had tears in her eyes as she said, 'It will always be with me, Matei. You don't have to look after me any more. You can be free, live your life in the city – give your heart to another.'

Matei looked at Jana. 'Tell her to come with us,' he begged his alpha.

Jana shook her head, troubled. 'If Emilia's drawn to this place, then she should stay here. Let her try it. It doesn't have to be forever.'

'We will watch over her,' Aran promised him. 'If she's not happy, I'll bring her back.'

Matei pulled Emilia to him, touching his forehead to hers. He was trying not to cry. He couldn't believe what was happening.

'You walked through fire for me,' Emilia whispered.

'And I'd do it again. Every time. This is *not* goodbye,' Matei told her, struggling to get the words out.

'Never goodbye,' Emilia promised. '*Ever.*'

She hugged him, hard.

Twenty-One

'You *said* you were only going to be a day!' Kay said, when Jana and Katrina finally reappeared at the flat. 'I've had the police out, everything! I've had to lie to your mum and dad!' Kay put her hands on her hips. 'You've got beans and I want them spilled. What went down?'

'Just what we said,' Katrina insisted. 'A camping trip that went wrong. Mud. Grass. Wet . . .'

Kay shook her head. 'Really? And both of you had no signal and ran out of battery?'

'Well – I'm off to bed,' Jana said, edging out of the door.

'And I need a hot chocolate. How about one?' Katrina asked Kay.

Kay sighed and shrugged. 'Why not?'

Katrina dumped her stuff on the counter and started bustling around the kitchen, which gave Kay the perfect opportunity. She nabbed Katrina's phone and found the last app that was used. It was the video camera. She opened it and it immediately began to play a clip.

'. . . *and they think they're dogs*!' squeaked Katrina's

terrified voice, loud and tinny from the phone. Kay hurriedly turned the volume down.

'What was that?' Katrina asked, from the kitchen.

'Nothing!' Kay said quickly, her eyes fixed on the screen.

She stared in horror as she watched. Teeth, fur, eyes . . . It was awful – horrible! And Katrina had been right in the middle of it! Her friend obviously needed help, and that meant only one thing.

The Three Ks *had* to get back together.

Katrina was fast asleep when two figures in black broke into her room and loomed over her bed. She woke up with a gasp when one of them put their hand over her mouth.

'Nice PJs,' observed the intruder.

'Kara!' Katrina sat up, confused. 'What are you doing here?'

'We're here to rescue you!' declared her friend in a loud whisper, trying to drag Katrina out of bed. 'Come on!'

'Rescue?' Katrina repeated groggily. 'From what?'

Kay was stuffing Katrina's clothes and make-up into a duffle bag. 'We saw the video,' she said quietly. 'You can't stay here.'

That woke her up. She leapt out of bed. 'The *video*? How did you –'

'No time,' said Kara, already at the bedroom door. 'Every second we spend here, we're in danger from –'

She opened the door as she was speaking to find Jana standing in it, yellow-eyed, her skin veined with black. Kara and Kay screamed, dropping Katrina's things.

'Back off, or else!' Kara said shakily, brandishing Katrina's hair straighteners.

'Yeah, we know what you are!' Kay added.

Jana looked over their shoulders at Katrina. 'What did you tell them?'

'We saw the video on her phone,' said Kay.

'What video?' Jana asked.

Katrina cringed. She'd forgotten it even existed! 'At full moon, when you . . . I might have had my phone on, and . . .' She trailed off at Jana's look of utter disbelief.

'We're going to take Katrina and go,' said Kara. 'You don't hurt us, we don't hurt you.'

'No one's going to hurt anyone!' Katrina told them. 'Jana's my friend.'

'Friend?' Kay said, incredulous. 'She's not even human!'

'You're right,' Jana said. 'I'm not human. But I'm not a monster either. I'm not going to hurt Katrina. Or anyone.'

'Katrina's still coming with us,' Kay told her.

'No, I'm not.' Everyone looked at Katrina, surprised. 'Come back in the morning,' she said. 'But right now you're going home, and I'm going back to bed.'

'They're not going anywhere,' said Jana, fixing Kay and Kara with her most terrifying wolf look. 'Phones.

Now.' She advanced on the two scared girls slowly, letting them see her teeth.

'Jana, come on,' said Katrina, 'stop mucking around!'

Jana kept going until she was right in their faces. Kay snapped, thrusting her phone out with a shaking hand. Kara followed suit.

'So much for being a nice werewolf,' Kara said sarcastically.

'I said I wouldn't hurt anyone. Never said I was nice,' Jana reminded her. 'And I'm a Wolfblood, not a werewolf.'

She deleted the duplicated videos from both phones and passed them back. Kay and Kara left at a flat run, not even stopping when Katrina called after them.

'Why would you even do that?' Matei asked, in horror.

'You must have known the video would get out!' Selina added, just as horrified.

They were all in the Kafe. Katrina and Jana had kept it closed for a morning so they could work out how to deal with this new problem.

'I didn't know Kay and Kara would steal it!' Katrina said, tearfully. 'And I've deleted it now, I really have!'

Matei snorted in disgust. 'And how long before they tell everyone what we are?'

'We need you to speak to Kay and Kara,' Jana told Katrina. 'Get them on our side. Get them to agree to keep the secret. They trust you. All you have to do is tell them the truth: we're not a danger to anyone; we just want to be left in peace. Text them now. We'll get the Kafe open.'

'All right,' said Katrina miserably. 'I'll try.'

Kara and Kay agreed that they would meet Katrina, but only if they could choose where. They picked a coffee shop on the other side of town, a popular place about three times the size of the Kafe, as if Kay and Kara wanted to make sure there would be plenty of witnesses.

'Hi, girls,' Katrina said tentatively, as they both stood up to face her when she came in. 'Can we . . . talk?'

Kay and Kara looked at each other. Then they grabbed Katrina by an arm each and pulled up her coat sleeves.

'Hey – what are you doing?' Katrina protested.

'Checking for bites,' Kara told her, as she looked at Katrina's neck. 'For all *we* know, she's turned you.'

'That's not how it works,' Katrina explained, pulling away gently. 'You get born a Wolfblood, not bitten.'

'Really?' Kay asked doubtfully.

'They don't want to cause any trouble,' Katrina tried to tell them, as they sat down and ordered coffee. 'They're people. With hopes and dreams, and skateboards . . . and really, *really* bad dress sense . . .'

'And you're all . . . friends?' Kay said in disbelief.

'Oh yeah,' said Katrina. 'They're always in the Kafe and hanging out in the flat. TJ's going to –'

'TJ's one as well?' Kay asked.

Katrina nodded. 'And Selina. And Matei. And Matei's sister, she's adorbs! And –'

'And they're everywhere,' Kara shook her head. 'Well, that's all nice and cosy, isn't it? You and your *pets*.'

Kay winced. 'Kara, I know this is weird, but –'

'This is how they get you!' Kara went on. 'They're all friendly and fluffy, and next thing you know, they invite you for lunch and *you're* lunch!'

Kay shook her head. 'I don't think that's –'

'They're werewolves!' Kara hissed.

'Wolfbloods!' Katrina corrected her, getting annoyed now. 'Are you even listening?'

But no, Kara wasn't listening at all. She'd made up her mind. 'Look at all the things that happened in Stoneybridge! Maddy, Rhydian. And what about Tom and that hypoglycaemia? His eyes went yellow. If you have to be born one, what was happening to him, eh?'

Kay saw her point. 'So – they lied to Katrina!'

'They lied to everyone,' Kara said, scornfully. 'And as for Shannon and her "Beast of the Moor" . . . It was Segolia that offered to pay Shannon's way through college. The company that Doctor Whitewood's working for!'

Kay frowned. 'You think they're Wolfbloods, too?'

Kara nodded. 'It's a Wolfblood Mafia!'

'Girls,' Katrina tried, but Kara interrupted her.

'We have to look out for you,' her friend told her. 'Just the same way we always have.'

222

Something about Kara's words made Katrina shiver. 'What do you mean, look out for me?'

Kara crossed her arms, a satisfied smile on her face. 'We've made sure you never have to be scared of her again.'

Katrina actually felt her heart stop. 'Kara,' she said slowly. 'What have you *done*?'

Imara was staring in despair at the big screen in her office when TJ, Jana and Matei walked in. All three of them stopped dead as they realised what she was watching. It was phone-camera footage of the forest just outside the wild Wolfblood camp. The full moon was clearly visible overhead, and beneath . . . well, beneath was an entire pack of Wolfbloods, transforming. As grainy and shaky as the film was, that was crystal clear as the sounds of howling and Katrina's terrified voice emanating from the tape.

This was bad. This was exceptionally, extremely bad.

'Congratulations,' said Imara quietly, once the film had ended. 'For the first time in my long and distinguished career, I'm literally speechless. YouTube, Tumblr, Instagram, Reddit . . . It's *everywhere*.'

Jana's shoulders sagged. 'I thought we'd dealt with it.'

There was something about Imara that looked utterly defeated. Somehow that was even scarier than if she'd been angry. 'You *knew* this existed, and you didn't tell me?'

'It's not Jana's fault,' Matei said, stepping in.

'We dragged Katrina to the wild,' TJ added. 'If anyone's responsible, it's us.'

'TJ, go home and pack,' said his mum. 'I've booked us a flight. A car will come to take you to the airport. I'll meet you once I've covered our tracks here.'

TJ took a step back. 'Whoa, Mum. You're Segolia. Why do we have to run?'

Imara shook her head. 'Because I never told anyone here that my son ran off to the wild pack and took a human with him! Go. I'll be right behind you. I booked for Antigua, like I promised for your birthday. Sun, sea and sand . . .'

TJ looked at Jana, who smiled back as brightly as she could. 'No one can run alone,' she said, trying to make it easy for him to leave her. 'Imara's going to need you.'

'What about you?'

Matei and Jana looked at each other. Jana reached out and squeezed Matei's hand. 'We'll leave the city. Go to the wild,' she said, before looking back at Imara. 'They'll come for Katrina, won't they? She'll have to come with us.'

Imara nodded. 'Go, TJ.' She grabbed hold of her son and wrapped him in a fierce hug. She seemed on the verge of tears. As she watched Imara hold TJ close, Jana realised just what was about to happen.

'Go check the coast is clear,' she told Matei softly.

Once he and TJ had left the office, she turned back to the Segolia alpha. 'You're not going, are you?'

Imara shook her head. 'I can buy enough time for TJ to get away. And you. But only by staying myself.'

'You can't just send him away on his own,' Jana said, desperately.

'Listen to me!' Imara said urgently. 'TJ is all that matters to me. He's my world, and no one is going to harm him. Ever.' She grabbed a piece of paper and scribbled something on it before handing it to Jana. 'This is where to contact him in Antigua. He'll be with good people. Family.'

Jana reluctantly took the address. 'Imara –'

'You're the alpha now,' Imara interrupted. 'Go, and don't look back. And tell him . . . I tried my best.'

'You can still make it,' said Jana, but Imara cut her off with a swift shake of her head.

'Go!'

Jana looked at Imara for another moment. Then she nodded in respect. They were both alphas, doing what they had to do to protect their pack. Jana promised to herself there and then that she'd do whatever she had to do to keep TJ safe for Imara.

Twenty-Two

Selina knew something was wrong as soon as she walked through her front door. Her mum was sitting in the living room, staring at her laptop. It only took Selina a second to work out what her mum was watching.

'What?' she asked, shocked. 'Where did you –'

'Everyone's talking about it,' her mum said, her voice grave. 'It has half a million views already.'

Selina's heart almost beat right out of her chest. She felt sick. She pulled her phone out of her pocket, but her mum grabbed her wrist before she could call TJ.

'Selina, you were lucky you're not involved in this,' said her mum. 'We need to keep it that way. Stay home, keep your head down for a few days.'

'No!' Selina exclaimed. 'I need to warn them. They're my *pack*!'

'You can't help them,' said her mum. 'Not against Segolia. Not against this.'

'But I can't just abandon them!'

'The damage is done,' said her mother softly. 'And they wouldn't want you getting into trouble. We need you right here, with us, where we're safe.'

Selina stared at her mother for a moment. Then she nodded and put her phone back in her pocket. She went up to her room, but she didn't stay there.

She'd learned how to climb out of the window long ago.

'Jana!' Katrina said, as she, Jana and Matei met outside the Kafe. 'They put it online!'

'I know. Katrina – you're in danger,' Jana said. 'You'll be fine, but you have to come with me. *Right now*.'

'Where?' Katrina asked. 'I'm not going back to that forest again!'

'Katrina!' Jana called, as her friend marched straight into the Kafe.

Jana and Matei followed, as agitated as Katrina was. Inside, all three of them stopped dead. The Kafe was surprisingly busy, but the biggest surprise was that it was busy because Mr Jeffries seemed to have become some sort of idol. He was standing surrounded by teenage girls, all asking questions as he signed their copies of *Bloodwolf*.

'But it's all true, isn't it?' one of them twittered. 'I saw the video that proves it!'

Jeffries struggled away from his fans as soon as he saw Jana. He came over, a worried look on his face. 'Downloads are through the roof. Everyone's talking about a video. *What* is going on?'

'I was just about to ask you the same thing, Mr Jeffries.' The voice came from behind them. They all turned to see a young woman with a notebook and an eager smile on her face. 'Zuhra Chakrabati, *City Herald*. Answer a few questions about this video?'

Jeffries looked flustered. 'Well, I'm a bit busy . . .'

'You know it has upwards of a million views now?' said Zuhra. 'Some people say it proves your book is based on real events. Real live werewolves.'

Jeffries laughed nervously, with no idea of what to say. That didn't seem to bother the journalist, who ploughed on regardless.

'Your friend Doctor Rebecca Whitewood works for Segolia now, doesn't she?' said Chakrabati. 'One minute she's fired for obsessing about werewolves. The next, she's head of research at a major multinational.'

Jeffries cast about for something to say. 'She's . . . very talented.'

'So was her predecessor at Segolia, Alex Kincaid,' Zuhra observed. 'Funny thing is, he's completely disappeared. He had a thing about werewolves too . . .'

The journalist raised her eyebrows, expecting him to say something. Jeffries just looked like a rabbit in the headlights. Jana knew she was going to have to step in. She looked over to Jeffries' fans, still whispering excitedly among themselves . . .

. . . and just like that, the solution occurred to her.

228

'You want an interview?' she said, suddenly. 'I'll tell you *everything*.'

Jeffries and Matei looked at her as if she was mad, but Jana ignored them. She gestured to a table and they all sat down.

'We made the video to promote Mister Jeffries' book,' Jana said. 'To build up a bit of excitement. Is it real or isn't it? People love that stuff.'

Matei got what she was doing immediately. 'We didn't realise how fast it would spread,' he chimed in.

Jeffries nodded enthusiastically, but the journalist didn't seem convinced.

'It's a remarkable video for a teacher and some teenagers,' she said. 'No offence. Crudely shot, but those special effects . . .'

'It's amazing what you can do on computers these days,' Matei said, smiling hard.

'What about Doctor Whitewood's involvement?'

'She's a very close friend of mine,' said Jeffries. 'And a respected biologist, which gives it a sense of authenticity.'

'She even borrowed equipment from work, to make it look more real,' Jana added.

Zuhra nodded, making notes. Jana and Matei glanced at each other. They couldn't tell if they'd fooled her or not. Then she looked up at Matei.

'Your sister Emilia is in the video. Is she around today?'

'She's . . . at home,' Matei said uneasily.

'That's odd,' said the journalist. 'Your foster parents said she'd moved away.'

Matei panicked. 'Her new home,' he said. 'With . . . relatives in Romania.'

Zuhra raised an eyebrow. 'Must have been hard. Losing her parents. Now she's been torn away from her brother –'

'No one tore her away from anyone!' Matei burst out. 'She wanted to go!'

Jana grabbed his hand, trying to calm him down as Matei began to vein up.

'This is a family matter, Ms Chakrabati,' said Mr Jeffries firmly.

The journalist smiled. 'That's what I thought the police would say. But they're treating this as a "missing person" case . . .'

Jana was getting increasingly worried about Matei. He wasn't holding it together at all. 'We have to go,' she said shortly, and dragged him out of the Kafe.

'Jana,' Matei said, walking quickly away from the café as he struggled to control his wolf. 'We have to disappear, right now.'

'I can't do that. Katrina needs protection.'

'So bring her!' They stopped beside the river and Matei turned and grabbed her hands, looking at her fiercely. 'It's over here for us. We go to the wild. Both your packs unite. You and me. Together.'

Jana felt her heart racing. If she had a choice, she'd do what Matei was suggesting in a flash.

'I can't,' she said, heart thumping painfully. 'But that doesn't mean you shouldn't go.'

Matei shook his head. 'And leave you here with all this?'

'Someone needs to warn the wild pack,' said Jana. 'Go, tell my dad what's happened. Keep your sister safe. I'll come find you.'

'And if the pack go into hiding?'

'I can always find my pack,' Jana promised him, with a wide smile that she tried to feel on the inside as well as the outside. 'Always.'

They pulled each other into a hug, holding on tightly. For a moment, Jana wished she could forget about anything except the feeling of being in Matei's arms – warm, wanted. But she was an alpha. She had responsibilities that she could not walk away from.

She pulled away and forced another smile. 'Go,' she whispered.

Matei touched his forehead to hers for a moment, and then nodded. He stuck his hands in his pockets and walked away. Jana turned to look out at the sun glinting on the river, trying to quell the urge not to let him go, to follow him, grab him by the hand and run with him into the wild.

Jana didn't see the black car race along the road

towards him. She just heard the screech of its tyres as it pulled to a halt and then Matei's yell.

'Matei!' Jana shouted, spinning to see a Segolia security team leap out and grab him. She launched into a frantic run as they bundled him into the car, but it was too late. Matei disappeared from view behind black windows and the car pulled away, too fast for her to do anything.

Jana heard hurried footsteps behind her. It was Selina, running towards her at full pelt.

'They're coming after you next, aren't they?' she asked as she slid to a halt beside her alpha.

Jana nodded, too close to tears to speak. Selina hugged her hard. Then they both had the same horrible thought.

'TJ!'

TJ was becoming increasingly worried. He'd packed all his stuff and his mum's too, but she still hadn't got home. She said she'd booked a cab, and if she didn't hurry, she'd miss it. Maybe she was planning to meet him at the airport? He'd tried her phone again and again, but it just went through to voicemail.

He heard a car pull up outside and dialled his mum's number again. 'Mum! Cab's here! Call me!'

He hung up and the phone rang in his hand. It was Jana. TJ answered it as he gathered his bags and walked down the hall to the front door. 'You heard from my mum?' he asked. 'She's not –'

'Segolia took Matei,' Jana said, cutting him off.

'What?' TJ asked, shocked, holding his phone to his ear with his shoulder as he opened the door.

'Watch your back,' Jana told him. 'Make sure the cab is –'

The front door swung open. On the step stood a man and a woman, dressed in sharp black suits with earpieces fitted to their ears. They weren't cab drivers. They were Segolia security. TJ dropped the phone, kicking his suitcase into their path as he ran back through the house. If he could make it through the kitchen and to the back door he could get across the garden and lose them by jumping the wall and escaping into the forest beyond.

He made it out of the door and ran for the stone steps that led to the lawn, way ahead of his attackers. TJ ran across it and threw himself at the high wall at the end of the garden, scrambling up and over. He jumped down and for a second he'd thought he'd made it. But then another figure appeared – a huge Wolfblood also dressed in black and also fitted with an earpiece. TJ tried to ram his way past, but the guard was built like a colossus. He held TJ back as the other two appeared.

He was surrounded and outnumbered. He was caught.

'I think they've got him,' Jana told Selina, still clutching her phone to her ear.

Selina was already running before Jana had chance to

say anything else. She was fast, even for a Wolfblood, so maybe she could make it . . . She ran full tilt to TJ's house, only pausing when she saw that the door was open. Selina stopped, sniffing cautiously before she went inside. The house was quiet. TJ's scent trail led through the house to the kitchen, where there was a chair turned on its side. The French windows were open. Selina went out into the garden, but there was no one there. The only sign of TJ was his sweatshirt. It was lying in a heap on the ground. It looked as if it had been torn off him – there were claw marks all over it.

Selina picked it up slowly, her heart clenching hard. She realised there and then that if anything had happened to TJ, she wouldn't know how to cope. Somehow, slowly and without her really even realising it, he had become very, very important to her.

Selina pressed his sweater to her face, feeling tears pricking at her eyes.

They came for Imara next, although they didn't have to look very far to find her.

The Segolia alpha waited quietly in her office while the security guards approached. Then she stood up and went out with them of her own accord. To anyone watching it would have seemed like someone walking to their execution.

*   *   *

Jana went back to the Kafe. She was so preoccupied with worry for her pack that she didn't even notice that it was shut. She tried the door, then realised that the whole place was empty and dark. Frowning, Jana pulled out her keys and opened the door, stepping cautiously inside.

There was no one there at all. No sign of Katrina or her dad. Jana walked through the empty premises slowly and paused at the bottom of the steps that led up to the flat. This was a trap, she knew it, and yet she had to go upstairs. What if Katrina was being held hostage up there?

Jana sniffed as she climbed the stairs. That scent . . . she knew that scent.

She followed it into the darkened living room. There was a figure sitting in one of the armchairs. As Jana entered, it reached up a hand and flicked on the light.

'Hello, Jana,' said Victoria Sweeney. 'I need your help.'

Twenty-Three

Victoria Sweeney, head of Segolia security, was sitting calm as you like in Jana's front room. Jana hadn't seen the woman since she had helped to stop Kincaid from de-wolfing the wild pack. Sweeney was hard and unyielding in her determination to protect the Wolfblood secret at all costs and her tactics were often harsh. Jana knew that Sweeney would do *anything* to keep the secret from the human world. She also knew that it would have been Victoria Sweeney who ordered the kidnapping of Jana's entire pack.

Knowing this didn't make Jana very inclined to listen to anything the woman had to say.

'We locked down the problem,' Sweeney told her, calmly. 'They're safer with us than anywhere else.'

'They're my *pack*!' Jana shouted.

'One pack,' Sweeney pointed out. 'You're *one* alpha. What protects all our kind? The secret. Always the secret.'

'They would never betray Wolfbloods,' said Jana angrily.

Sweeney smiled coldly. 'And yet, here we are. The only way to save your friends is to protect our secret,' she insisted. 'You and I – together.'

'How?' Jana asked, still suspicious.

A noise echoed up from the empty café downstairs. Sweeney tensed. 'Who's with you?'

'It's just Selina,' Jana told her, recognising her scent. 'She's probably looking for TJ.'

Sweeney raised an eyebrow. 'TJ? Bring her up. We can use her.'

Jana went downstairs. She held a finger to her lips before Selina could say anything. 'When I say run, we run,' she whispered.

A second later they burst out of the Kafe, running for their lives.

Jeffries, Katrina, Kara and Kay had been locked in a Segolia waiting room for hours. Since Kay and Kara seemed intent on having a go at both Katrina and Jeffries for lying to them about the existence of Wolfbloods, the wait was even more unpleasant than it could have been. So much so that when Sweeney finally arrived to talk to them, it was immediately clear that they were all completely over this whole illegal imprisonment thing.

'Why are you doing this?' Jeffries demanded. 'You've got no right to keep us all prisoner!'

'You're my guests here,' she told him. 'For the moment. We all have a problem and I'm here to fix it. Just like old times, Mister Jeffries.'

'What do you want?'

'A simple public statement. Then everything goes back to normal. Better than normal. You help us . . . and we'll help you.'

'You? Help me?' Jeffries asked, confused.

'We have a medieval archive in need of a historian,' Sweeney told him. 'You'd never have to teach again . . . or write bad novels.' She turned to Kara and Kay. 'Further education is so expensive these days. Our scholarship fund would cover it all. We'd pay off your debts. Assist in your career development.' Finally she looked at Katrina. 'And we would of course invest in your . . . Kafe. Help you expand the brand nationwide.'

They all looked at each other. 'And if we don't co-operate?' Jeffries asked.

'Do you really need to ask me that?' Sweeney raised her eyebrows.

Kara shrugged. 'We agree.'

'Sure,' added Kay. 'If it gets us out of here.'

Sweeney smiled. 'You've made the right choice.'

'Wait,' said Katrina. 'What about Jana? And TJ and Matei – where are they? If you want us to cooperate, you'd better tell us what's happening to them. *Where's Jana?*'

Victoria Sweeney's next stop was Imara. She had the former Segolia alpha brought back to her own office in the custody of one of the guards Imara used to command

– just so there was no confusion about who was now in charge.

'I understand your situation,' Sweeney said, getting up from where she had been sitting comfortably at Imara's desk. 'If I had a son who had made a mistake, I might have hidden it from the rest of us, too.'

'Where is he?' Imara asked, her face steely.

Sweeney paused for a moment. 'Carter Hall.'

Imara knew exactly what that meant. She snarled, wolfing out as she tried to leap at the other Wolfblood, but the security guard held her back.

'You really think teeth and claws are going to fix this?' Sweeney asked. 'Give me a *reason* to spare TJ.'

Imara pulled herself free of her guard's grasp and stared at Victoria with yellowed eyes. 'What kind of a reason?'

Sweeney smiled slightly. 'Jana has a den somewhere in the city.'

'I don't know where it is,' Imara said immediately.

'TJ does,' Sweeney pointed out. 'Get him to tell us and you can both go home. Untouched. Do we have an agreement?'

Imara let her wolf fade as she thought. She didn't want to do this, but what choice did she have? TJ was her *cub*. Reluctantly, she nodded.

'Take her to her son,' Sweeney told the guard. 'I'll be there shortly.'

'Miss Cipriani?' the guard said, quietly, one hand on Imara's elbow.

Imara stared at Sweeney for a moment, then turned and walked out of the office she'd spent so many hours in, trying to keep her kind safe, out of the building she'd helped to protect. She felt numb. This *had* to work. She couldn't allow TJ to undergo Protocol 5, she just couldn't. Not her cub. He was so young, so full of promise – and he'd only experienced his wolf once. Whatever deal she had to strike, Imara knew she'd agree to it, whatever the cost.

Outside, a viciously cold wind sliced across the car park. Imara pulled the collar of her coat up around her ears as the guard shepherded her towards a car. Imara was so caught up in her thoughts that it took her a moment to recognise the familiar scent blowing towards them. Her guard growled. Then, just a split-second later, Jana and Selina were upon them.

Selina attacked the guard with shocking speed, knocking the key out of the woman's hand with enough force that it sailed into the air and was deftly caught by Jana. Selina struggled to hold the guard back as Jana went to Imara.

'Imara, start the car!' Jana urged, opening the driver's door.

Imara hesitated.

'Imara!' Jana yelled, holding the driver's door open. 'Come on!'

Imara hung back for another second, then ran to the driver's door and got in, starting the engine as Jana jumped in the other side. Selina held the guard back until the last possible moment, then pushed her captive away and threw herself into the back seat. The three of them roared away from the Segolia offices as if the hounds of hell were on their tails.

They headed for Carter Hall, but parked a little distance away. Imara led them through the woods surrounding the facility instead.

'Victoria's plan,' Jana demanded, as they walked. 'What is it?

'Protocol Five,' was Imara's answer – as if it told them anything at all.

'What *is* Protocol Five?' Selina asked.

'No more lies,' Jana added, her voice determined. 'Tell us. *Now.*'

Imara grimaced. She knew they weren't going to like the answer.

TJ and Matei had been locked into a barred cell. It was distinctly less comfortable than the room the Three Ks and Jeffries had been left in. There were only hard bunks to sit on in the narrow room, the walls were rough brick and a bare light bulb hung from the arched ceiling.

They had been there for hours. At first they had tried to find a way out, but the bars had obviously been constructed to withstand Wolfblood strength. There was no way to escape. All they could do was sit and wait.

They both leapt up, wolfing out as the sound of footsteps echoed towards them from the gloom outside their cell. Just beyond the iron bars were steps leading up out of sight; on these a small figure appeared, moving down them slowly and deliberately.

It was Carrie Black.

'Hello,' she smiled sweetly, pressing her face to their bars. 'I was asked to come and talk to you about your treatment.'

'Treatment?' TJ repeated, with a growl.

'What treatment?' Matei asked, baring his teeth.

Carrie didn't seem at all bothered by their anger. 'It's the freedom to be the person you should have been,' she said. 'It's freed me. I'm different now. Happier!'

'I don't understand . . .' said Matei.

'I think I'm starting to,' TJ said, staring at Carrie.

'The anger,' the girl went on. 'The fire burning inside. It's . . . gone. No more terror. No more pain. No more *animal*. Just me. You can be cured, too.'

'We're going to be de-wolfed,' TJ said, his worst fears confirmed. 'That's what Protocol Five means!' He clutched the bars, appealing to Carrie. 'We don't need "curing"! It's not a disease, it's what we are!'

'You want this thing inside you?' Carrie asked. 'Doesn't it just burn you up inside?'

242

'Er, let me think,' TJ said sarcastically, before yelling, 'No!'

'That's not the wolf,' Matei added. 'That's *you* hating yourself!'

Carrie was starting to get agitated. 'It's the wolf,' she insisted. 'It's evil. It makes you do terrible things . . .'

Matei threw up his hands. 'Like what? What could you have done bad enough for them to do this?'

Carrie shook her head, obviously upset. Behind her, footsteps echoed and Victoria Sweeney appeared, coming down the stairs flanked by two of her goons – and Doctor Whitewood.

'You think you can take our wolves as easily as you took hers?' Matei snarled, pressing himself hard against the bars of the cell. 'Come and try!'

'You don't understand, Matei,' said Sweeney, her voice completely calm.

'I understand enough. You're evil.'

'Am I?' Sweeney smiled. 'We took her wolf for her own good. It's what she wanted.'

'She's just a kid,' Matei protested. 'How could you –'

'Because she killed your parents.'

At first he didn't even understand the words. Matei froze, staring at Sweeney, who was looking at him with a strange kind of triumph. Slowly he turned to Carrie, who was cowering beside Doctor Whitewood. It couldn't be true. Could it?

'It wasn't my fault,' she began. 'Segolia sent me to your dad for counselling. He said I could learn to love the wolf. He transformed to show his wolf wouldn't hurt me. But it freaked me out. I could feel my wolf rising, trying to get out. I panicked, knocked things over. Something caught fire. I don't know how, I just . . . ran.'

TJ looked between them, as shocked as Matei. '*You* killed Matei's parents?'

'The *wolf* did!' Carrie cried.

It was too much for Matei. He went beserk, raging at the bars as if he could tear them apart. TJ only just managed to hold him back.

'Thank you, Carrie. You can go,' Sweeney said. They all watched her leave, climbing the stairs slowly with her head bowed. 'We do what we have to. For Carrie. For the secret.'

'You stopped Kincaid,' TJ said, to Sweeney and to Whitewood, too, who waited in the corner. 'You were heroes! And now you're using his research on us?'

Becca looked upset, but there was no sign of remorse on Sweeney's face.

'We're organising a press conference,' she said. 'Jeffries will say the video is an online promotion for his book. And you two will provide blood samples for testing – proving that you are entirely human.'

'Yeah?' said TJ, sick of this. 'And what if I tell those reporters everything?'

Sweeney shrugged. 'You could. Or you could think about the Wolfbloods your sacrifice will keep safe. Like your sister, Matei. She's in the video. You'll do this for her, and the rest of the wild pack. And as for your mother, TJ . . .'

'My mum didn't know!'

'Well, she should have!' Sweeney snarled. 'So. Are you going to help me keep the secret or not?'

Twenty-Four

Sweeney's guards took Matei and TJ to a small room that Doctor Whitewood had set up as a laboratory. Two pristine white medical couches dominated the space. The two young Wolfbloods stopped dead as they were pushed inside. There was no way out. They were outnumbered. They were trapped. This really was the end.

'Lie down, please,' Becca said quietly, not quite looking at either of them.

Matei and TJ glanced at each other. Matei shook his head slightly, a defeated look in his eyes. What could they do? The safety of every Wolfblood they knew – and millions that they didn't – rested on their shoulders. Matei slid on to one of the couches as TJ hesitated.

'Oh well,' said TJ, as he lay down at last. 'At least I got to wolf out once in my life . . .'

Doctor Whitewood turned around with one of the serum applicators in her hand. She went to TJ first. From her face he could tell she wasn't happy about what she was being asked to do, but it didn't look as if she was going to stop. Becca turned TJ's head sideways, pressing the syringe to his neck. TJ gripped the arms of the couch, preparing for the needle to pierce his skin . . .

Victoria Sweeney's phone rang. She answered it. It was Imara.

'Wait,' barked Sweeney to Doctor Whitewood. 'Talk to me,' she said, into the phone.

'I've got Jana and Selina here. I'll bring them in,' Imara said, on the other end of the line. 'If our offer stands.'

'Agreed.'

'We'll come in through the old tunnel network,' Imara told her.

Sweeney hung up, then looked at Becca. 'Don't do anything yet,' she said. 'Come with me,' she said to the rest of her guards, motioning that just one should stay.

As they swept out of the room, Whitewood backed away, looking relieved.

'How can you do this?' TJ asked her, as she put the syringe back in its box.

'I don't have a choice, TJ,' said the scientist, her voice quiet. 'And this will protect all Wolfbloods.'

Matei barked a harsh laugh that had nothing to do with humour. 'And the end justifies the means, is that right? Because that always works out well, doesn't it?'

Doctor Rebecca Whitewood turned away.

Imara breathed a guilty sigh of relief as she hung up. Selina and Jana were still in the woods, standing at the entrance to the tunnel she had led them to. Imara had known full well that it would be covered by a locked metal gate that would need tools to break open. There was a wrench in the boot of the car, and she'd needed an excuse to come back alone. It was the only way she could think of getting away from the two girls that would give her time to call Victoria Sweeney without arousing Jana and Selina's suspicions.

Imara had just betrayed them both, and she'd done it without a second thought. She'd had to. It was the only way to save TJ from Protocol 5. Now, whatever else happened, TJ – and TJ's wolf – would be safe.

Imara took a deep breath as she slid the phone back into her pocket. Then she got out of the car, found the wrench and set off back through the woods, still trying to ignore the sick pulse of guilt building in her gut.

'Are you OK?' Jana asked, as she caught up with them.

Imara nodded, but she didn't smile. 'I'll be fine just as soon as I've got TJ back,' she said quietly, fitting the wrench to the metal gate and preparing to lever it open. 'Here – I'll need to you pull . . . Pull!'

The gate resisted, but finally gave way, springing open to reveal a dark stone tunnel leading down into earth.

'You go in,' Imara told Selina and Jana. 'I'll shut the gate behind you.'

Jana nodded, trusting her completely. A moment later,

the two girls were making their way deep into the tunnel. Imara swung the gate shut, watching as they disappeared into the gloom. Then she raced back to the car and headed for the main gates of Carter Hall.

The tunnel that Jana and Selina found themselves in was dark and cramped. They felt their way forward along a stone floor that hadn't had anything walk over it for decades. Jana moved as quickly as she could, her wolf vision allowing her to see in the dark. She was frantic – she had to save TJ and Matei from Protocol 5. She couldn't be too late, she couldn't . . .

When Imara had told her exactly what Protocol 5 was, Jana had been so shocked that at first she couldn't believe what she was hearing. Taking someone's wolf away? What kind of Wolfblood could do that to another, whatever the reason?

'And you let them do this to Carrie?' Jana had asked, horrified.

'Carrie needed it,' Imara had said. 'But we have to save TJ and Matei before it's too late.'

Jana had had no choice but to agree, but once this was over – once Matei and TJ were safe – she was done with Segolia forever. Nothing could defend taking away a Wolfblood's birthright. Nothing.

She saw a flicker of light up ahead, the tunnel still dim but growing brighter. They were almost there. Jana quickened her pace, turning one more corner and seeing the passageway open out in front of her.

'We're in!' Jana announced to Selina as they burst out into an empty cellar.

Except that the cellar wasn't empty at all. In seconds she and Selina were surrounded by Segolia security guards, yellow-eyed and ready to fight. Victoria Sweeney stood in front of them, her arms crossed.

Worse still, though, Imara was there. She lunged forward and caught Jana by the wrist, twisting her arm behind her back.

'How could you do this?' Jana shouted, struggling uselessly against Imara's strong grip.

'They have TJ,' said Imara simply. 'What choice did I have?'

'Jana!' TJ gasped, as she was manhandled into the laboratory with Selina close behind her. 'Selina!'

Matei took Jana's hands. 'Are you OK?' he asked. Jana nodded, a look of utter defeat on her face.

Then in walked Victoria Sweeney. Imara was at her side. TJ could not have been more shocked.

'Mum?' TJ whispered.

'TJ,' Imara said, walking to him quickly. 'You're safe now. You're coming home with me.'

'What?' TJ asked, horrified as he realised what she must have done. 'Mum – no!'

'You're safe now,' she said again. 'Come on . . .' She tried to grab his arm, but TJ jerked himself away from her grasp.

'Don't touch me!'

'TJ,' said Jana. 'Go. It's OK.'

'No,' he said, looking his mother straight in the eye. 'I'm staying with my pack.'

Imara looked frozen with shock, but Victoria Sweeney didn't hesitate.

'Doctor Whitewood,' she ordered, gesturing to the young Wolfbloods. 'Who's next?'

'TJ, just go,' Selina begged. '*Please.*'

'Yeah,' Matei agreed. 'Go on. Get out of here.'

TJ's attention was still on Imara. 'How could you do this?' he asked her. 'How could you *possibly* think this is right?'

Imara moved as if she were about to grab TJ again – but at the last minute she pivoted and lunged at Doctor Whitewood instead. Snatching the syringe of serum, she pushed the scientist away and spun. Grabbing hold of Sweeney, Imara held the syringe to the security chief's neck.

'Back off,' Imara snarled at the guards.

'This doesn't help TJ,' Victoria told her, caught in Imara's iron grip.

'When I want parenting lessons from you, I'll ask. Until then, are you ready to sacrifice your own wolf? Or

251

will you let us go?' Imara pressed the syringe harder against Sweeney's neck.

Sweeney struggled for a moment, then gave up. 'Let them through,' she told the guards.

Imara hustled backwards with Sweeney in her grip. Jana and the pack followed, the rest of the guards surrounding them, snapping and snarling but keeping their distance. They made it out of the building and headed beneath a large stone arch to the car park. Imara's car stood in one corner.

'I'll take her,' said Jana, reaching for the syringe that Imara held at Victoria's neck. 'Everyone get into the car!'

Sweeney tried to squirm away from Jana as the guards made a lunge for the escaping Wolfbloods, but Jana's grip on the syringe didn't waver. She watched as everyone got into the car with Imara at the wheel. Selina and Matei climbed into the back seat, leaving room for Jana.

'This doesn't change anything!' Sweeney told them. 'Segolia will track all of you down. It's inevitable. You know that.'

'No,' Jana said into her ear. 'I'll take your serum, do your press conference. Whatever you want. Just as long as you leave my pack alone. This pack – *and* the wild pack.'

Sweeney stopped struggling. 'Agreed,' she said.

'Jana, come on,' Matei urged, as Imara gunned the engine.

'Jana!' Selina shouted.

'Jana, get in!' yelled TJ.

Jana kicked the car door shut. 'Go!' she shouted to Imara.

'Jana – no!' Matei shouted.

Matei scrambled to get out, but Imara hit the child lock, sealing all the doors. He hammered on the window, shouting for Jana.

'Imara!' Jana bellowed. 'Get them out of here!'

Imara's car roared away as TJ, Selina and Matei struggled to get out. Jana waited until they were through the gates, then she dropped the syringe. A minute later, she was surrounded.

This is for the pack, Jana told herself, as she was dragged into the laboratory and strapped to one of the beds. *This is what an alpha does. Whatever the cost, she protects her pack.*

It didn't make her any less terrified. Or any less heartbroken. She remembered what had happened to Meinir when Kincaid's serum had robbed her of her wolf.

Without my wolf, what will I be? Jana wondered. She didn't want to think about the answer.

Jana realised that Sweeney was speaking.

'You will be the stuff of legend, Jana. The wild Wolfblood alpha who sacrificed her wolf to save our secret. We salute you.'

Sweeney actually had the audacity to give the Wolfblood bow, even as Doctor Whitewood approached with the serum. Jana clenched her jaw, defiant as she looked the scientist in the eye.

'I am so sorry,' said the scientist, her hand shaking slightly as she injected Jana with the serum.

Jana felt it burn through her veins like fire. She winced, jerking against her restraints. She thrashed on the gurney, her mouth stretching into a wide, silent scream.

Sweeney watched Jana's pain for another moment, and then turned away. 'Bring them both to me at the press conference as soon as she's ready,' she ordered one of the guards as she left.

TJ, Selina and Matei tumbled into the pack's secret den with Imara close behind them. Matei was distraught.

'I should have been the one to stay,' he said. 'It's my sister she threatened.'

'Jana's our alpha,' Selina pointed out. 'She did what had to be done for both her packs.'

'Human or not, she stays our alpha,' said TJ, as the three of them huddled together. 'She did this for us, for *all* of us.' He pulled away after a few moments, turning to see Imara watching them. 'Mum, I'm sorry. For what I said. You were the Trojan horse . . . wolf! Cunning and smart, pretending to be on Sweeney's side.'

'I wasn't pretending,' Imara told him.

'What?' TJ asked, shocked. He felt Matei and Selina tense beside him.

'You wouldn't come,' Imara said simply. 'You wouldn't abandon your pack. So I had no choice but to save you all. You can hate me for it, but when you have your own cub you'll understand.'

'But . . .'

'There are no buts,' she told him. 'I'd sacrifice a thousand packs for you.'

Before TJ could say anything else, there was a sound at the entrance to the den. They all tensed as footsteps came closer. Had Segolia found them? But the scent was very familiar . . .

Matei was moving in a second. He rushed towards the figure that walked into the muted light. It was Jana, black veins tracing through her skin, her eyes yellow.

Her pack stared at her in mute shock.

'Jana?' Matei breathed. 'You're still . . .'

'A Wolfblood,' Jana said, smiling.

Matei grabbed her, pulling her into a tight hug and holding her as if he'd never let go. Jana shut her eyes and clung to him.

'But – how did you fool them?' Selina asked, amazed.

'I think you'll find *I* fooled them,' said another voice, as Becca appeared. 'Worst thing about being a scientist,' she added. 'Everyone always takes credit for your work.

Though Jana *is* the one who locked our guard in a broom cupboard, so . . .'

TJ shook his head, confused. 'So are you going to explain, or do we stand here with our mouths open all night?'

Whitewood smiled. 'I gave her the same serum I gave to Meinir. Nice dramatic reaction to fool Victoria – but no harm done to her wolf-self.'

Jana pulled away from Matei, grinning as she looked over at Selina and TJ. 'I didn't know until afterwards. I –'

Whatever else she was going to say was drowned out by Selina and TJ both throwing their arms around her in a giant group hug. Jana laughed as Matei joined in, too. They all held on to each other as if they'd never let go, and Jana had rarely been so happy in her life. Her pack, reunited. Could anything ever be better than that?

It was Imara who brought them back to earth.

'So what happens now?' she said. 'We can't hide down here forever.'

'That's why we need to end this,' Jana replied. 'Once and for all.'

'But how?' Selina asked. 'What can we do?'

Jana took a deep breath. 'The only thing we can.'

The press conference was in full swing. It had been staged inside the huge glass-and-steel foyer of the Segolia building, where a stage and table had been set up for the speakers. In front of the stage were rows and rows of chairs, and every one of them was taken. There were journalists from all over the world gathered to hear what Segolia had to say about the video. There were cameras and recording equipment of all sorts. Zuhra Chakrabati was sitting right in the front row, listening carefully.

Mr Jeffries was speaking, flanked by the Three Ks. Sweeney watched proceedings from the edge of the stage. She'd been very clear about what Jeffries and the girls should say, and she was pretty certain they wouldn't deviate from the script. They were all too scared – and besides, they all had too much to lose.

'The video was an online promotion for my novel, *Bloodwolf*,' said the teacher. 'I had no idea it would be so popular . . .'

'Mister Jeffries was our teacher, so of course we said we'd help with his video,' added Kara, as cameras flashed, snapping picture after picture.

'The idea was, we'd post it online as if it was real,' Kay explained. 'Because if he did it himself, it'd be too obvious.'

Victoria Sweeney looked around, then summoned one of her guards. 'Whitewood should be here with Jana by now,' she hissed. 'Call her.'

The guard returned a few moments later. 'Doctor Whitewood's not answering her phone.'

'So where are the teenagers who actually feature in this video?' Zuhra asked.

Sweeney took to the stand herself. 'We do have one of those appearing in the video coming right now to provide a blood sample,' she said. 'Unfortunately –'

She was interrupted by one of her men. He dashed on to the stage and grabbed her shoulder, whispering urgently into her ear. Sweeney froze. Surely she hadn't heard him correctly. The acoustics in the room must be playing havoc with her hearing, because she'd thought he'd just told her that there were five wolves outside . . .

Sweeney stood up abruptly. The journalists began to stir.

'What's going on?' asked Zuhra Chakrabati.

A ripple passed through the crowd as Victoria Sweeney left the stage. There was some sort of commotion occurring at the back of the room. The entire press conference had begun to turn around, straining out of their seats to see what was happening. Some of the journalists began to shout. Those with cameras rushed to shoot film and take photographs.

Then, for the first time in her life, Victoria Sweeney found herself genuinely terrified.

Five wolves walked calmly into the building. They were beautiful creatures with glossy fur and large paws, and they pushed through the glass doors of Segolia as if they knew exactly what they were doing. The wolves took no notice of the humans who were now frantically trying to get a clear view while simultaneously backing away in fear. The wolves skirted the edges of the gathered press, not rushing, simply walking calmly to the front of the room.

One of them leapt gracefully on to the stage and then on to the table holding the microphones. It turned to sit at its centre, looking out at the amazed crowd and giving everyone a chance to take as many pictures as they wanted before leaping back to the floor. This wolf – and it was clear to everyone there that this must be the natural leader of the pack – landed in the centre of the line that had been formed by the other wolves.

Then, in front of everyone – in front of every camera and every journalist – they began to change. Their fur became skin and hair, their eyes lost their yellow glow, and they moved to stand on two legs, instead of four.

They became Jana, TJ, Selina, Matei and Imara.

They became . . . *human*.

There was a moment of complete and utter silence as the assembled journalists struggled to believe their eyes.

Victoria Sweeney stood to one side, consumed by an utter and abject horror.

'You want the truth?' Jana said, addressing the room with absolute confidence. 'Well – here we are.'

And that was when the room went mad.

* * *

259

Much, much later, once the pack had answered as many questions as they could and the news of the proven existence of Wolfbloods had ricocheted right around the world, Jana and the others made their way back to the Kafe with Katrina, Becca and Jeffries. There, Katrina and Jana cooked enough food to feed about ten hungry wild packs, and they all sat down together and ate, like a family. There was a party atmosphere, even though they all knew that nothing would ever be the same again. The world knew about Wolfbloods now. It wasn't a terrifying secret they had to hide every second of every day.

There was a bang at the door. Katrina went to answer it and found Kay and Kara outside.

'You two?' Katrina said, coolly. 'I'm surprised you want to be seen with us.'

'Yeah, well – we wanted to check you were all right,' said Kara.

'Look, Katrina,' said Kay. 'We're the K's. Nothing will ever change that.'

Kara nodded, looking past Katrina to the others. 'We're . . . sorry,' she said, loud enough for them all to hear. 'For posting that video. We were just looking after our friend.'

Jana looked at them both for a moment. Then she nodded. 'There's nothing more important than that.'

'Apart from protecting your family,' TJ added, looking at his mum.

'Or pack,' Selina pointed out.

'All right,' Jana corrected herself. 'There's nothing more important than friends, family and pack. I'm the alpha round here, you're supposed to agree with everything I say!'

TJ grinned. 'Wouldn't that be boring?'

As Kay and Kara joined the party, Jana's phone rang.

'Don't answer it,' Matei told her, putting his hand over hers. But Jana had seen the name on the screen. It was Victoria Sweeney.

'I have to,' Jana said, as she put her phone to her ear. But she didn't let go of his hand. Instead, she laced her fingers between his. Matei smiled at her and stroked his thumb over her knuckle.

Sweeney had told Jana that they needed to meet. She chose the viewing platform of the BALTIC Centre for Contemporary Art, after dark. She and Jana stood side-by-side, looking out at the glittering lights of Newcastle. The Tyne Bridge stood like an iron guardian over the rippling water.

'Segolia's finished,' Sweeney told Jana. 'The share price has flatlined, the Wolfblood employees have mostly fled. We can't protect anyone any more.'

'Lies don't protect anyone,' said Jana. 'They make us turn on each other. Humans can learn to accept us.'

Victoria grimaced. 'I hope you last long enough to see that day, Jana. Because right now, you and your friends are the most visible Wolfbloods in the world. That's a responsibility, a weight – and it will make you a target. Maybe this is the end of everything. Wolfbloods in cages, repression, rebellion, even war . . .'

Jana's stomach clenched. She didn't want to think that could happen. 'I have to believe in a better world,' she said. 'Why did you want to see me?'

'To warn you,' was the reply. 'It's not humans who'll come after you. There are Wolfbloods who'll never forgive you for what you've done. Keep your pack close, and watch your back.'

With that, Sweeney slipped away, leaving Jana alone.

The wind whipped around Jana as she looked out over the vibrant city she had made her home, wondering what the future was going to bring. Whatever Victoria Sweeney's fears about what might be coming, Jana still knew she had done the right thing. Secrets and lies were no good for anyone. She had to trust that there was a future where Wolfbloods and humans could live together side by side, in peace. Didn't her own pack prove that it was possible? Katrina, Becca, Jeffries – and now even Kay and Kara – they were all part of her pack now, all part of her family, and they would stay that way for good: taking care of each other, putting each other first.

Jana needed to believe that what she had achieved with her own pack was possible for all Wolfbloods, for all humans. She just had to lead the way towards that future.

That was her purpose, she realised. That was what had called her away from the wild. That was why she was here – and why she would stay.

No matter what.

WOLF BLOOD

Hungry for more?
Don't miss these . . .

Maddy has a secret. She is a Wolfblood.
But could there be others?

AVAILABLE NOW

Rhydian's pack are back. Can he and
Maddy resist their dark power?

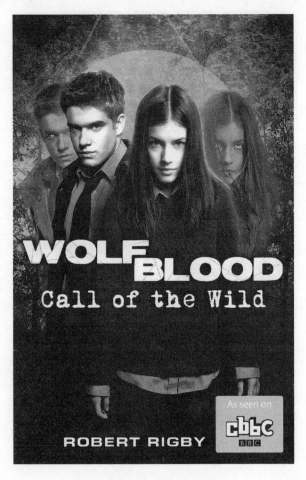

AVAILABLE NOW

Can they stay together when their
world is falling apart?

P R E S S

Thank you for choosing a Piccadilly Press book.

If you would like to know more about our authors, our books or if you'd just like to know what we're up to, you can find us online.

www.piccadillypress.co.uk

You can also find us on:

We hope to see you soon!